"I Know Exactly What You Were Thinking About Right Now," Ike Said Softly.

"I've seen that look often enough on a woman's face. You were thinking about having something, all right, but it wasn't dinner."

Annie narrowed her eyes. "Boy, you have got some ego. Food was exactly what I was thinking about. I was thinking that the breast of chicken in Ike sauce...I mean *wine* sauce...would be really good. For dinner."

Ike chuckled. "I see. I can only imagine what you have in mind for dessert."

"Cheesecake," Annie said, without looking at him.

"Funny, that's what I'm planning to have, too."

"Well, you'll have to get your own," she assured him. "Because I'm not sharing mine with you."

Dear Reader,

It's hard to believe that this is the grand finale of CELEBRATION 1000! But all good things must come to an end. Not that there aren't more wonderful things in store for you next month, too....

But as for June, first we have an absolutely sizzling MAN OF THE MONTH from Ann Major called *The Accidental Bodyguard*.

Are you a fan of HAWK'S WAY? If so, don't miss the latest "Hawk's" story, *The Temporary Groom* by Joan Johnston. Check out the family tree on page six and see if you recognize all the members of the Whitelaw family.

And with *The Cowboy and the Cradle* Cait London has begun a fabulous new western series—THE TALLCHIEFS. (P.S. The next Tallchief is all set for September!)

Many of you have written to say how much you love Elizabeth Bevarly's books. Her latest, *Father of the Brood*, book #2 in the FROM HERE TO PATERNITY series, simply shouldn't be missed.

This month is completed with Karen Leabo's *The Prodigal Groom*, the latest in our WEDDING NIGHT series, and don't miss a wonderful star of tomorrow— DEBUT AUTHOR Eileen Wilks, who's written *The Loner and the Lady*.

As for next month...we have a not-to-be-missed MAN OF THE MONTH by Anne McAllister, and Dixie Browning launches DADDY KNOWS LAST, a new Silhouette continuity series beginning in Desire.

Lucia Macro

Senior Editor

Please address questions and book requests to:
Silhouette Reader Service
U.S.: 3010 Walden Ave., P.O. Box 1325, Buffalo, NY 14269
Canadian: P.O. Box 609, Fort Erie, Ont. L2A 5X3

ELIZABETH BEVARLY
FATHER OF THE BROOD

Published by Silhouette Books
America's Publisher of Contemporary Romance

For Gail Chasan and Lucia Macro,
who make doing my job a real pleasure.
Thank you both.

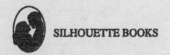 SILHOUETTE BOOKS

ISBN 0-373-76005-1

FATHER OF THE BROOD

Copyright © 1996 by Elizabeth Bevarly

ELIZABETH BEVARLY

is an honors graduate of the University of Louisville and achieved her dream of writing full-time before she even turned thirty! At heart, she is also an avid voyager who once helped navigate a friend's thirty-five-foot sailboat across the Bermuda Triangle. "I really love to travel," says this self-avowed beach bum. "To me, it's the best education a person can give to herself." Her dream is to one day have her own sailboat, a beautifully renovated older model forty-two footer, and to enjoy the freedom and tranquillity seafaring can bring. Elizabeth likes to think she has a lot in common with the characters she creates, people who know love and life go hand in hand. And she's getting some first-hand experience with maternity as well—she and her husband recently welcomed their first-born baby, a son.

Dear Reader,

Someone once asked me why I thought romance novels were so wildly popular, and, for a moment, I was stumped for a response. Then I realized it's because romance novels are one of the few things in our society that are so specifically tailored to women. Almost exclusively, women write, edit and read romance. The heroines in our books are strong, savvy and sensual. Too often in our society, women are discouraged from being such things, but in a romance novel, there's always a gorgeous, intelligent man who prizes a woman for those very traits. Talk about your happy endings...

And those happy endings are what it's all about. Romance novels are often dismissed as insubstantial fluff. But those of us who love them know that simply isn't true. Over the years, a good deal of change has come to our genre. And Silhouette Books has always been the front-runner of promoting that change, especially in its Desire line. I've enjoyed Desire novels that depict everything from time-travel to single-parenting to overcoming substance abuse to recovering from domestic violence. So much for insubstantial fluff.

A romance novel is just about the only place a woman can visit where the world works the way it's supposed to, where good people are rewarded for their good deeds, and nice guys never finish last. In romance novels, no matter how tough a woman's life gets, by the last page, we know she's going to be just fine. And in this day and age, with the society we have to meet head-on every day, what woman wouldn't be attracted to that?

There's nothing better than a good romance. That's something Silhouette knows, and something the Desire line has always aspired to bring its readers. I'm proud to be a Desire author *and* a Desire reader. And I can't wait for the next 1000.

Best wishes,

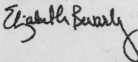

One

"This is the most ridiculous thing I've ever done in my life. I don't know how I let you talk me into this."

Ike Guthrie gazed at his sister's reflection in the cracked, spotty mirror and frowned. Nora Guthrie stood behind him, reaching over his shoulders to straighten his black bow tie. Behind her, a chorus of characters and a cacophony of voices split a haze of white cigarette and cigar smoke. Nora gave his tie one final tug, a gesture that nearly cut off his breath. He frowned again.

"Why is it, big sister," he grumbled through gritted teeth as he loosened the knot that had nearly strangled him, "that you've always been able to talk me into doing things I don't want to do?"

She brushed her palms down the smooth, satiny lapels of his tuxedo and smiled with much satisfaction. "It's a talent I inherited from Mom. There. You look fabulous. You're going to bring top dollar tonight. If you don't win the grand prize, there's no justice in the world."

Ike eyed her warily. Like he, Nora was well above average in height, but her five-foot-ten still only brought her to his chin. Like his, her white-blond hair was fine and straight, but where hers was wound into a sleek French twist, his was razor-cut short and stylish. Their blue eyes, too, were a perfect match, right down to the overly long lashes. He glanced at their formal attire and frowned yet again. He looked like a fool in this monkey suit. God almighty, how had he let Nora talk him into this?

"Top dollar?" he repeated, turning to face her fully. "You talk like I'm some prime cut side of beef."

Nora brushed a speck of lint from his shoulder. "Tonight, dear brother, you are. And all we on the board of St. Bernadette's Children's Hospital care about is how much you bring per pound."

He opened his mouth to reiterate his reservations about this whole affair, but a loud commotion beyond a curtain on the other side of the room halted his objection. All the other men present in the room also paused to listen, each of them wearing an expression of undisguised panic. As if drawn by an invisible thread, Ike moved to stand next to the curtain, lifting his hand to pull it slightly to the side so that he could look past it.

Beyond was a stage surrounded by hundreds of women, each clutching a fistful of dollars. At the moment, those women seemed to be uncommonly pleased by whatever unfortunate man was up for grabs, because they hooted and whistled and cheered as if the home team had just come in for another unchallenged touchdown.

"Two thousand dollars!" Ike heard the auctioneer shout out in delight. Her voice was feminine, loud and rabid. "Going, going, gone! Well, ladies, that's the highest bid we've received so far tonight. Looks like Dr. Gillette might just take home the grand prize."

"Phooey," Nora muttered beside his ear. "They haven't gotten an eyeful of Isaac Guthrie, Philadelphia's most prominent architect."

Ike shook his head as more wolf whistles erupted from outside. "Something tells me they're not going to care too much about what I do for a living," he said softly.

Nora made a face at him. "I know that. But you've got a great tush, Ike. I'm telling you, your choice loins are going to bring in a fortune."

Dr. Gillette came through the curtain then, dabbing a handkerchief at a forehead that was glistening with perspiration. "They're animals," he gasped. "Absolute animals. I don't even know who bought me. Two women in the front row nearly came to blows."

Nora patted his back comfortingly as he passed. "Don't worry, Dr. Gillette. I'm sure whoever purchased you is a perfectly nice woman." She lowered her voice as she added to Ike, "It was probably Edith Hathaway. She said she was determined to buy a doctor for her daughter, Pamela, no matter what the cost. And hey, if you ask me, a cardiologist for two thousand bucks is a steal."

"Our next bachelor up for bids" came the auctioneer's voice from the other side of the curtain, "is Mr. Isaac Guthrie, one of Philadelphia's most prominent architects and most desirable men. I'm sure you've all admired the new Bidwell Corporate Center downtown. Well, Mr. Guthrie designed it. In addition to his architectural acumen, Isaac enjoys horseback riding, the poetry of Lord Byron and moonlit walks along the beach...."

"No, I don't," Ike whispered to his sister. "I've never ridden a horse in my life, and I hate poetry. Where's she getting all that stuff?"

"Shh," Nora quieted him. "There's more. I wrote it myself."

"*You* wrote it? But, I gave them a different—"

"Shh."

His sister silently mouthed the rest of his introduction as the auctioneer offered it. "He's a Scorpio, thirty-six years old, a gourmet chef and excellent tennis player, who sees his dream woman as someone who's smart, sensitive and has a great sense of humor...."

Ike expelled a sound of disgust. "That's *supposed* to read 'someone who's small, sexy, and has a great set of hooters.' I thought it might keep anyone from buying me."

"I know, you jerk. That's why I changed it."

He sighed. "Just wait, Nora. Someday, somehow, I'll get even."

"Shh."

The auctioneer continued. "And the date Mr. Guthrie is offering is an overnight weekend extravaganza!"

More catcalls and whistling indicated the crowd was very enthusiastic about the announcement, not to mention digging deeply into their pocketbooks.

"'Weekend extravaganza?'" Ike repeated incredulously. "I told them it was going to be dinner and a show. Where's this all-night stuff coming fr...?"

He looked at his sister. Nora was smiling. "I told you you're going to bring top dollar." She rolled her eyes at his expression. "Oh, quit pouting. I've taken care of all the arrangements for you. All you have to do is show up." Her smile became devilish. "Hey, it's not like you can't afford it, Mr. Moneybags. And it's for charity, after all, Ike. Just remember that some deserving children are going to get the medical treatment they wouldn't get otherwise because of you. Thousands of dollars worth of medical treatment if I have anything to say about it."

"Obviously, I don't have anything to say about it, do I?" Nora shook her head.

"Even though it's *my* choice loins that are on the block?"

"Shh. You might just be bought by the woman of your dreams."

"I doubt that." He sighed, resigned to his fate. "Oh, well. I guess I should be happy that you at least got the part about my being a Scorpio right."

The auctioneer had by now finished describing the overnight excursion to Cape May, New Jersey—her tone of voice carrying just the right amount of dubiety when she mentioned the separate rooms at the Hanson House Bed and Breakfast—and was lingering over the catered sea-food brunch on the beach. Ike was shaking his head in wonder at his sister's imagination and almost missed his cue. Then Nora shoved him hard from behind and he had no choice but to stumble out onstage.

"This is the most ridiculous thing I've ever done in my life. I don't know how I let you talk me into this."

Annie Malone stared at her older sister, wondering how on earth Sophie always managed to get her to do things she normally wouldn't even dream of doing. A bachelor auction. Honestly. Even if it was for charity, Annie had a million other things she should be doing tonight.

"Shh," Sophie told her, glancing down at her program. "Look, this guy is perfect for you. He loves horses and Byron, *and* he knows how to cook." She threw her sister a look of censure. "And seeing as how your idea of boiling water is putting it in the oven and setting the temperature at two-hundred-and-twelve degrees, this could be the beginning of a beautiful relationship."

"I don't want a relationship," Annie told her petulantly, "beautiful or otherwise. Mark was—"

"I know," Sophie cut her off. "Mark Malone was the man of your dreams, the heart of your heart, and you'll never find another love like him again. But Mark's been dead for five years, Annie. It's time to get on with your life."

Annie flinched at her sister's matter-of-fact mention of her dead husband. Yes, Mark had been gone for a long time now. But she couldn't possibly forget about him as quickly as Sophie evidently had. Nevertheless, she countered, "I have gotten on with my life. Quite nicely, in fact. I don't want or need a man in it."

"Yes, you do," Sophie assured her with another quick scan over the new bachelor's vital statistics. "And I'm going to buy you one. It's the whole reason I insisted you come with me tonight. It's the only reason I came myself."

"I thought it was because you think St. Bernadette's Children's Hospital is a deserving charity."

Sophie waved her hand at her as if Annie had just made a quaint little joke. "Silly. Come on, get an eyeful of this guy. He's exactly the kind of man you need. You want him and you know it. And I think you should have him."

Before Annie could say a word in protest, Sophie lifted her hand at the auctioneer's request for three hundred dollars. She lifted it again when the bidding went to five hundred. And again when it went to seven hundred. And then to one thousand. And two thousand. Annie didn't try to stop her sister, simply because she couldn't believe Sophie was going to go through with it. Then she reminded herself that her sister was everything she wasn't—assertive, confident and married to lots and lots of money. If Sophie got it into her head that she was going to buy a man for Annie, then she would and could sit here and bid all night.

When Sophie started to raise her hand in agreement to a bid of three thousand dollars, Annie grabbed her wrist in an effort to stop her. But Sophie only raised her other hand instead, and shouted out, "Five thousand dollars!"

"Five thousand!" the auctioneer repeated on a gasp. "My goodness, Mr. Guthrie, you *are* greatly desired." She tittered prettily at her double entendre.

For the first time, Annie took a moment to consider the man her sister seemed determined to buy for her. She glanced up onto the stage to find that the bachelor in question was very tall, very blond, very well groomed, very good-looking, and, as all the other bachelors up for bids had been that evening, doubtless very wealthy. In other words, he was everything she *didn't* want in a man. As she opened her mouth to warn Sophie to knock it off *right now,* Annie noticed that the bachelor onstage was also staring back at her sister without even trying to mask his unmistakably sexual interest in her.

And that was when Annie really got mad.

Okay, she couldn't fault a man for looking at Sophie like…like…like *that,* but this guy was about to burn down the building with his incandescent gaze. So what if Sophie's henna-stained auburn hair and pale green eyes caught the edge of the spotlight as if born to it? So what if her sapphire evening gown was virtually cut down to her navel and nearly every body part sparkled with gems? So what if her bright red smile suggested any number of unearthly delights? So what?

So why couldn't the man onstage look at Annie that way, too?

The question exploded in her brain before she even knew what hit her, and for the life of her, she could understand none of it. Helplessly, she looked down at her own modest, long-sleeved, black cocktail dress, and at the simple, sandy-colored braid that fell over one shoulder nearly to her breast. Almost unconsciously, she brushed a hand over the pale freckles on her nose and cheeks that had survived her adolescence along with her well-scrubbed, gee-whiz complexion. And although she did have green eyes like Sophie's, Annie's were rounder and less remarkable without the added enhancement of shadow.

All in all, she knew she looked like the wholesome, sensitive kind of woman a man would want to talk to about the other women in his life. Other women who could very easily include her own sister. Annie had been through that scenario often enough, after all.

Of course the man onstage would be looking at Sophie, she told herself without an ounce of envy. What man wouldn't? Who cared if he was ignoring Annie and focusing on her sister as if Sophie were the answer to a prayer? Annie wasn't interested in him anyway. If it wasn't for the fact that Sophie was already happily married, she would wish her sister and the bachelor the best. Unfortunately, Sophie's five grand wasn't paying for a man for Sophie. It was paying for a man for Annie. And maybe that was what was really making her angry.

"Sophie, you don't have to buy me a man," Annie told her sister in a grim whisper. "I can find one for myself. I mean, I *could* find one, if I wanted one. Which I don't."

"Not like this one, you couldn't," Sophie countered. "Not working with the kind of people you work with."

"Underprivileged children," Annie reminded her sister, trying to tamp down her irritation. "I work with underprivileged children."

"Exactly. Which means you couldn't meet a decent man to save your life. The men you meet are all social workers and family counselors and public servants and the like."

"In other words, decent men."

"That's not the kind of decent I mean and you know it. You don't need a *decent* man, Annie. You've got all the decency you can handle in that overgrown, do-gooder heart of yours. What you need is an *indecent* man." She smiled mischievously. "The more indecent the better." She nodded toward the bachelor onstage. "Just look at that guy's nether regions. He's going to be perfect for you."

Annie declined her sister's instructions and looked at the man's eyes instead. They were cool, distant and still fixed on Sophie. "Even if he likes Byron?" she asked absently.

"Especially if he likes Byron. Byron was pretty indecent himself, you know."

"Yeah, I know. I minored in English, remember?"

Instead of answering, Sophie nodded with satisfaction at the auctioneer's announcement of "Going...going... gone for five thousand dollars!"

"Come on," she said as she tugged on Annie's sleeve. "Let's go get your man."

"He's not my man," Annie said, remaining seated steadfastly in place. "You bought him. He's yours."

Sophie smiled wryly, "And what am I supposed to tell Philip?"

Annie shrugged. "Tell him you're going to lovely, romantic Cape May for the weekend with one of Philadelphia's most prominent architects and indecent bachelors."

Her sister gazed at her mildly. "And then Philip will divorce me. Is that what you want?"

She shrugged again. "You're the one who bought Mr. Wonderful up there, not me. I'm not going anywhere with him."

Sophie stared at her sister for a moment through slitted eyes, as if she were carefully considering her options and thoroughly unwilling to let five grand go to waste. Because, naturally, Sophie would consider a charity donation an unnecessary expense. Then Sophie began to smile. A decidedly evil smile that Annie didn't like one bit.

"So what you're telling me," Sophie began, "is that I just paid five thousand dollars for an attractive, successful, intelligent man who is going to take you to spend the night in one of the most beautiful towns in the United States, and that you refuse to go."

"That's right," Annie told her. "I refuse to go."

"How about if I bribe you?"

Annie narrowed her eyes suspiciously. "What kind of bribe?"

"How about if I double the amount I just paid for him and donate it to Homestead House? Then would you go?"

Annie stood to meet her sister's gaze levelly at that. "Ten thousand dollars to Homestead?"

Sophie nodded, her smile growing broader.

"That's a low blow, Sophie."

"Yes, I know, but hey, it's tax deductible, right? Philip wouldn't care. He'd think it was a sweet gesture for me to make. Besides, it will work, won't it?"

Annie didn't have to think twice. Homestead House was a juvenile home that she and her husband had started ten years ago and that she had kept going after his death. She had met Mark Malone in college, where they were both studying social work. Upon graduation, they'd scraped together personal funds, found a few backers, and won a few government grants, and had pooled the money to buy an old, dilapidated house in one of Philadelphia's less-than-desirable neighborhoods. They'd brought it up to code, and had then turned it into a haven for kids who got lost in the system and had nowhere else to go, no one left to turn to.

Even during the best of times, Annie had to scramble to make ends meet and keep Homestead House open. Ten thousand dollars would buy a lot of the things she needed.

"Okay, I'll do it," she agreed. "But only because of Homestead."

Sophie shook her head in amazement. "Little Annie Malone," she muttered in the way that Annie had always hated. "Still thinks she can save the world from itself after all these years. Well, let me tell you something, little sister. Something I learned a long time ago. The world's a brittle, ugly place, and nothing you can do will ever change that. You better get yours while you can and enjoy it, and then watch your back. Because nothing in this life is worth much, but there's always someone who wants to take it away from you anyhow."

Annie nodded, not in agreement, but because this was the same philosophy Sophie had been spouting since they were adolescents. "Maybe that's what you believe," she said softly, "but I see things a little differently. You've got your life, Sophie, and I've got mine. As brittle and ugly as you think it is, I find it very rewarding."

Sophie smiled. "Not as rewarding as the one this guy could give you," she said. "Just you wait. One night with him, one little taste of the good life he has to offer, and you'll want more. And the more you see of his way of life, the more you'll like it. Just you wait, Annie. You're in for a treat. Once you've sipped his wine, you'll never go back to that crummy tenement you call home again. I guarantee it."

Sophie turned then to cut her way through the crowd and pay for her purchase, and Annie followed obediently behind. Her sister was wrong about her life and her life-style, Annie knew. But there would be no arguing with Sophie about that tonight. At the moment, all Annie cared about was the ten thousand dollars she'd be depositing into the Homestead account Monday morning. She decided to start her shopping list with athletic equipment and work her way through the alphabet to the zoo trip she'd always wanted to take with her kids but had considered too frivolous. By the end of the week, she thought with a smile, she was going to have some very happy children on her hands.

She would also be packing for a weekend that was certain to wind up being disastrous. Oh, well, she thought. Ten grand was ten grand. She'd walk over fire to get that much money for her kids. How bad could a weekend in Cape May be, even if her companion would more than likely turn out to be a jerk? If nothing else, the fresh ocean breeze would be a welcome change over the stale, stagnant city air she was so used to breathing. And it would be nice to walk along the beach again, moonlit or not.

Fresh air and a view of the ocean, she marveled as she watched Sophie carelessly write out a check for five thousand dollars and hand it to the cashier. Two things that brought pleasure without costing a dime. It was a lesson her sister could stand to learn, and, judging by the high price tag on his offered date, something the bachelor onstage might benefit from, too.

But it wasn't up to her to teach that lesson, Annie thought. It was only up to her to watch out for her kids. And like a protective female animal stalking the wild, she'd do whatever she had to do to make sure her brood was protected. Above all else, Annie Malone would always make sure her kids came first.

Ike breezed through the curtain and met his sister backstage feeling buoyant, lusty and full of anticipation. "I owe you," he told Nora as he embraced her fiercely. "I owe you big. Did you get a load of the woman who bought me?"

He felt Nora nod against his shoulder. "Oh, I got a load, all right."

Ike sighed wistfully. "I can think of no greater pleasure on earth than to be owned by that woman for an entire night."

"I told you it would all work out," Nora said when he released her. She twisted her mouth into a wry grin. "St. Bernadette's gets five thousand dollars, and you get that great set of hooters you wanted. Well, my, my, my. Isn't the world a lovely place?''

"Oh, Mr. Guthrie."

Ike turned to find his new owner passing through the curtain behind him as gracefully as she would if borne on wings. While he was onstage, he had been fearful that in good light some of her dazzle would diminish. But he'd been wrong. Good light only made the woman even more radiant. He didn't so much approach her as he was drawn to her. All he knew was that he couldn't wait to take her hand in his.

"Hello, Ms....?" he began as he drew nearer.

"I'm Sophia Marchand," she said as he reached for her hand.

But she stepped away before he could curl his fingers around hers, then thrust another woman forward to take her place—a drab, colorless creature who faded to nearly nothing beside her iridescent sponsor. Ike's gaze flickered over the newcomer for scarcely a second before returning to the woman who had launched a variety of previously undiscovered fantasies in his brain.

"And this is my sister, Anna," she told him. "I've bought you for her. She's so looking forward to the weekend you have planned. Enjoy."

And with that, the woman smiled and turned away, exiting through the curtain as quickly and completely as a magician's assistant disappears into the black beyond.

A mouse, Ike thought as he gave the other woman another quick once-over. His gorgeous peacock had bestowed upon him a mouse to take her place.

"Annie," the mouse said quietly. Her voice was huskier than he would have thought, but he got the feeling she would indeed squeak when she reached the proper decibel. "My name is Annie. Annie Malone."

She extended a hand toward him and smiled, a smile that was pleasant and harmless and rather pretty in a wholesome kind of way. In spite of her smile, however, Ike

somehow got the impression that she was no more pleased
by this turn of events than he was.

"Ike Guthrie," he replied automatically, taking her hand
in his.

Her hand was small, a bit rough, and in no way decorated. The woman who had bought him had been wearing
rings on nearly every finger, and he'd already begun to indulge in all kinds of salacious imagery about her long, red
nails. Annie's hands didn't evoke sensual pleasure. They
evoked hard work. And her eyes didn't promise untold
realms of erotic discovery. They suggested about as much
sexual expertise as an ingenue. Ike's gaze skittered lower,
and he sighed again. And great hooters, he noted with
much disappointment, were simply out of the question.

"Nice to meet you, Ms. Malone," he said as he met her
gaze once again.

Too late, he realized she understood completely where his
own eyes had been lingering. But instead of blushing and
turning away, as an ingenue would have, she had arched
one eyebrow and squeezed his hand hard in what he concluded was an unspoken threat.

"Please, call me Annie," she said, sounding surprisingly hardy in comparison to her slight build. "After all, we
will be spending the night together." The eyebrow fell, but
one corner of her mouth lifted in a sardonic grin.

Oh, goody, Ike thought. A weekend with Raggedy Ann's
evil twin, Craggedy Annie. He hadn't noticed at first that
big chip on Annie Malone's shoulder, and he didn't know
what caused it to sit there so resolutely. But now he could
see it clear as day. She might look sweet and innocent—hell,
she might look like a kid just freed from college—but there
was an angry energy barely coiled within her that was just
about to blow. Hastily, Ike dropped her hand before she
could drag him down with her, and shoved his own hands
deep into his pockets.

Oh, well, he thought further as he noted the sprinkling
of pale freckles that dotted her nose and cheeks. Maybe
some sun would give her a little more color. And the sea

breeze would be good for her. If it didn't blow her right into the ocean first.

He glanced over his shoulder to find that his sister had been paying close attention to the scene played out. Nora nodded her approval, lifted a hand to circle forefinger and thumb in *okay,* then left the room laughing.

Two

"*Annieee!*"

Annie sighed with much frustration and growled under her breath. Now what? she wondered.

The cry had come from Mickey, that much she could determine immediately. But the little guy had a six-year-old's propensity for wanting just about everything, and right away at that, and his cry of terror at the sight of blood was virtually identical to his urgent plea for just one more cookie. Whatever the problem was, Mickey, at least, would consider it of global importance.

Annie dropped her favorite pair of blue jeans on top of the meager wardrobe selections she was packing for the weekend and went in search of Mickey. She found him with his head caught between the rungs of the stairway banister and rolled her eyes hopelessly as she bent to help him free himself.

"I told you not to do this, didn't I?" she asked him calmly as she twisted his head carefully to the side.

"Yes," he whimpered, clearly frightened by his predicament but determined not to show it.

"The last time this happened, what did I say?"

Mickey sniffled. "I don't remember."

Annie's voice softened. "I said, 'Mickey, if you put your head in the banister railing this way, it's going to get stuck.' Isn't that what I said?"

"I guess so."

"So why did you do it again?"

He hesitated, biting his lip as Annie carefully extracted his head from the rungs. He remained silent as he stood rubbing his hands furiously over his forehead and through his pale blond hair. His blue eyes were resolute and adorably menacing.

"Well?" Annie prodded.

Mickey thrust his stomach forward, a gesture he probably thought she would find intimidating. Annie only smiled.

"I'm waiting," she said.

Mickey relaxed and looked down at his feet. "I don't know."

She nodded her understanding. "Okay, hotshot. Just try not to do it again, okay?"

He nodded back. "Are you still going away this weekend?" he asked as he followed her to her room.

"Yes." Annie went back to her packing, resigned to the Spanish Inquisition that she knew would follow. Mickey asked a lot of questions. And she'd discovered long ago that she had no alternative but to answer every one of them if she ever hoped to maintain any kind of balance in her life.

Mickey scrambled up onto her bed and began to remove things from her duffel bag, inspecting each item as if it were the most fascinating scientific specimen he'd ever had the good fortune to encounter. "Where are you going?" he asked.

They'd been through this a million times already, so Annie had the routine down pat. She continued to pack as she obediently replied, "Cape May."

"That's in New Jersey, isn't it?"

She nodded again. "Yes."

"And New Jersey is across the river, isn't it?"

"Yes."

He grinned, clearly pleased to be able to show her just how much he knew of the world. Then he plucked a pair of her socks out of the duffel, unrolled them and asked, "How long will you be gone?"

"I'll be back Sunday night."

"When will you be leaving?"

"Saturday morning."

"That's tomorrow, right?"

"Right."

"Who are you going with?"

"A friend."

"His name is Ike, right?"

"Right."

"And he lives in Philadelphia, like we do, right?"

"Right."

"Are you going to marry him?"

Annie stopped packing and gaped at Mickey. Well, that was a question that hadn't cropped up in their earlier interviews. Where on earth had he picked up an interest in marriage?

"Why would you think I was going to marry him?" she asked cautiously.

"'Cause that's what grown-ups do, isn't it? Molly says when you grow up and become an adult you have to get married. It's the law."

"Molly said that, did she?"

Mickey nodded furiously. "And she's older than me, so she knows what she's talking about."

Annie bit her lip. "Um, Molly's only seven, Mickey. She's not that much older than you."

"But she said grown-ups—"

"Not all grown-ups get married," Annie interrupted him gently. "Only the ones who fall in love."

The little boy thought about that for a moment, then asked, "Are you going to fall in love with Ike?"

She chuckled. "I can safely say no to that."

"Why not?"

She ruffled his hair. "Because he's not my type, kiddo."

"What's your type?"

Annie thought about her husband. She recalled Mark's unruly black hair and bittersweet chocolate eyes, his tattered jeans and sweatshirts, and how much he loved coaching little league baseball. She remembered how he had always talked back to the network news and secretly devoured true-crime books. She smiled as she reminisced about his expertise in bandaging scraped knees so the Band-Aid wouldn't pull, and about how he could bake absolutely perfect Toll-House cookies. And she realized she would never, not in a million years, meet another man like him.

"I don't have a type, Mickey," she said wistfully. "Not anymore."

Mickey nodded his approval. "Good. Because when I grow up, I'm going to marry you."

She smiled and bent to place a quick peck on his forehead. "Okay, palomino. I'll wait for you."

As quickly as he had taken an interest in her activities, the little boy's fascination abated. "I'm going outside," he announced as he launched himself off the bed. "See ya."

Annie watched him leave, marveling that such a sweet kid had come out of such a crummy situation. She knew she had no business picking favorites when she had ten kids ranging in age from six to sixteen living under her roof. But Mickey Reeser was Annie's favorite. No question about it.

She stuffed the last of her toiletries into the well-worn, army green duffel bag that had belonged to her husband, then placed it by her bedroom door. It was going to be a lousy weekend, she thought. Not only was she going to be spending it with someone she had no desire to get to know better, but she always became anxious when she had to leave her kids for any length of time.

True, she had two graduate students from local universities who volunteered part-time to help her out. But Annie was the one responsible for the children at Homestead House. She was the only human being in the world who was there for them twenty-four hours a day. She didn't like being gone overnight, even if Nancy and Jamal, her two volunteers, would be staying at the house with the kids. She just didn't feel right being away. She didn't feel as if she were being a good mother.

And although she reminded herself over and over again that she *wasn't* anyone's mother, she couldn't help but to have fallen into the role. The children of Homestead House had no parents or families, either because they had been orphaned or abandoned or worse. Annie was it for them. She was their mother, father, sister and brother. She was their role model, their caretaker, their rock. She was all they had in a world that had turned its back on them. And she didn't like leaving them alone.

Nevertheless, she reassured herself, it was only a weekend. Two days and one night that were of no consequence whatever in the scheme of things. And what could one simple weekend possibly do to screw up her very satisfying life-style?

Annie hummed as she closed her door behind her and headed down the stairs, an old Cat Stevens tune about the wild world. She decided not to dwell on the couple of days she'd be spending with Isaac Guthrie, prominent architect and indecent bachelor. Instead, she thought, she'd just look forward to Monday morning.

When her life would return to normal.

Ike glanced down at the piece of paper he had tossed onto the passenger seat when he'd climbed into his car that morning, then looked up at the red brick building again. Yep, this was the correct address all right. Though the place hardly looked habitable to him. There were bars on all the first story windows and a security door that was, at the moment, thrown open in welcome. The paint on the front shutters and door frame was stained and peeling, and what was left of the front stoop was a cracked, crumbling mass of concrete. A simple metal plaque affixed to the brick beside the front door read, *Homestead House*. And like everything else about the place, it looked old, tired and overused.

In contrast to the decay of the building—or perhaps in spite of it, Ike thought wryly—a bright cache of well-tended marigolds, petunias and geraniums had sprouted along the walkway that led to the sidewalk and street. They bestowed a certain humanity on the building it wouldn't have claimed otherwise, and he couldn't help but smile. The sky providing a backdrop for the place was blue and flawless, the warm spring afternoon balmy and full of promise.

If it wasn't for the fact that this was a remarkably bad neighborhood that no one in his right mind would choose to visit if he didn't have to, Ike might have seen some potential for the place. As it was, he couldn't for the life of him figure out what someone like Annie Malone was doing living here.

He had spoken to her briefly on the phone—once—since meeting her backstage the weekend before. The conversation had consisted of a few dozen words and lasted about a minute and a half. Mostly, they had just settled on what time Ike would pick Annie up and bring her home. And with that obligatory exchange out of the way, there had seemed nothing more to say.

Ike sighed. Man, he was dreading this.

He climbed out of his bright red sports car, eyed his surroundings and surreptitiously activated the car's alarm. He didn't plan on being here any longer than he had to, but in this neighborhood, his car could be stripped professionally in a matter of minutes. He scrubbed his palms over his khaki-clad thighs as he walked toward the front door of Annie's house, then checked his navy polo for any potential smudges of filth. He was beginning to feel dirty just being in the vicinity.

He was about to knock when the front door was thrown open wide and he was nearly overrun by children and hockey sticks. Without a notice or care of him, the kids went blustering into the street, shouting and prancing and scrambling for position. Ike was left shaking his head in wonder that children felt so utterly immortal that they didn't even watch for traffic. Then again, this street didn't look particularly well traveled, either, he thought as he glanced down one way and then the other. The realization was just something else that put him on edge.

"Hi."

He turned at the sound of a soft, husky, voice—a voice he'd heard on only two occasions, but one he was coming to find oddly familiar and comfortable nonetheless. Annie Malone stood at her front door wearing a white peasant blouse with roomy sleeves, very faded, hip-hugging blue jeans, and huge Birkenstocks on her otherwise bare feet. Her hair was parted in the middle and fell in two braids over her shoulders, and thanks to the thin, gauzy fabric of her shirt, he could clearly see that she was wearing an undershirt instead of a bra.

Ike didn't know why no one had bothered to inform Annie that the sixties had ended more than two decades ago, and he had to force himself not to impart the information to her himself. Instead, he decided he may have been a bit rash in dismissing her upper regions so easily last weekend. Although small, Annie had good form. Then he noted the exhausted-looking duffel bag at her feet that appeared to be more empty than full. Annie, it seemed, traveled even more lightly than he.

"I saw you from my window and decided to come down to meet you," she said. "I was hoping to make it before the kids trampled you, but..."

Ike glanced up when her voice trailed off, only to realize that she had once again been observing him as he ogled her. She had arched her left brow in that maddeningly challenging way, as if she were waiting for him to either assault her or offer an explanation for his rudeness. Ike did neither. He just tried to tamp down his irritation before it could become impropriety.

Hoping to defuse her anger, he glanced over his shoulder at the hastily scrambling children. "Do they all belong to you?" he asked. When Annie's gaze skittered past him to fall on the children, every ounce of animosity left her eyes, and her lips formed a fond smile. Ike knew then that inquiring about her children had been exactly the right thing to dissolve her exasperation.

"Yeah, they're all mine," she told him.

"Funny," he said dryly, "a couple of them look like they're in high school. You must have been about eight when you gave birth." Ike wanted to offer the further wry observation that Annie was in remarkably good shape for someone who had spent most of her adult life pregnant. But he refrained, fearing the comment just might put them back where they started—with him ogling, and her being ogled, and neither of them any too comfortable with the knowledge of it.

Her smile was still wistful when she said, "I may not have carried them inside me, but they still belong to me."

"So then you don't have any kids of your own?" Ike ventured.

She looked at him strangely for a moment. "Why do you ask? For some reason, you strike me as the kind of person who doesn't care much for children."

"That's because I *am* the kind of person who doesn't care much for children."

She sounded almost disappointed when she replied, "That doesn't surprise me. And no, I don't have any kids that are the product of any personal biological workings. But I do have kids. Lots of kids." Before he could ask anything more, she met his gaze again. "I'm ready to head out whenever you are."

Ike nodded. "Good. I didn't want to leave my car parked out here any longer than I had to."

She glanced past him at the bright red convertible and frowned.

"What?" he asked when he saw her disapproval of the sleek car he'd coveted for years before being able to afford it. "You don't want to drive to the coast with the top down?"

She shook her head. "Oh, I love the feel of the wind when I'm driving."

"Then why the sour look?"

"I was just thinking you probably paid more for that car than I spent buying and refinishing and outfitting this whole building."

This time it was Ike who frowned, wondering why he felt so damned defensive around this woman. "Yeah, I probably did. Real estate in this area isn't exactly prime—" He eyed her building deliberately before adding, "—or safe—for commercial or residential use. You know, my partner and I are working with the city on a beautification project that's leveling neighborhoods like this one and turning them into something useful."

She glared at him. "Neighborhoods like this one used to be the backbone of the city."

He smiled acidly. "Soon they'll be parking garages."

"And that's supposed to beautify the city?"

Ike looked around him again. "A nice, clean parking garage will be a damned sight more attractive than this...this..."

"Look," Annie interrupted him, "maybe you don't see much use for neighborhoods like this, but I see it in a way you obviously don't. Granted, the area isn't what it used to be, and yes, a bad element has begun to thrive. But there are still a lot of good people here. Besides that, it's affordable and suits my needs just fine."

Ike wanted to counter that if that was the case, then she was obviously and sadly neglecting her needs. But he kept his mouth shut. For the time being, he decided, he'd just as soon not wonder about Annie Malone's needs. She probably had way too many of them for any man to be able to

satisfy her. And why he should suddenly feel a tingling—
and not unpleasant—sexual awareness of her at the idea of
such, Ike couldn't begin to imagine. So he pushed the
thought away and bent to retrieve her duffel.

But someone else had beaten him to it, he realized before completing the action. Clutching the bag that would
be nearly as big as he was if it were full, was a young boy
with hair the mixed pale yellows of chicken noodle soup
and eyes so blue and large and guileless, they almost
stopped Ike's breath.

"I got it," the boy said as he stepped past Annie. "I can
carry it. Where do you want it?"

So transfixed was he still by the child's round-eyed expression that Ike could only thrust a thumb over his shoulder. The boy looked past him at the car parked at the curb,
and his huge eyes grew even larger with admiration.

"Cool!"

He slapped down the steps and stumbled down the walk,
weaving first one way and then the other under the weight
of the duffel. He dropped the bag by the trunk and, before
Ike could stop him, hauled himself over the side of the car
and into the driver's seat. Immediately the alarm erupted,
as loud and raucous as an air raid siren. And the little boy's
expression—the one that had been so utterly open and
carefree—transformed into a grimace of unadulterated
terror. When his gaze met Ike's, the boy actually began to
cower as if he were about to be sucked down into hell's
darkest core. Ike had never seen anyone look so scared before in his life.

"Hey, kid, it's okay," Ike tried to reassure him over the
noise.

He started down the walk toward the car, watching in
amazement as the little boy's fear grew more tangible with
every step he took. And when he rounded the front of the
car toward the driver's side and reached in to deactivate the
alarm, the little boy covered his head with his hands, curled
into a tiny ball and screamed.

Screamed as if his lungs were about to burst.

Ike could do nothing but stare dumbfounded as Annie calmly came up behind him, reached into the car instead and effortlessly plucked the boy out of the driver's seat and into her arms. He curled himself over her body as if he wanted to crawl inside her forever, then buried his face in her neck and began to cry with all his might. Annie patted his back and murmured soothing sounds until the boy's sobs abated some.

Then she looked at Ike with a perfectly normal expression and stated in matter-of-fact terms, "Mickey was badly beaten by both of his parents before he came to live with me. He thought you were going to hurt him for setting off the alarm."

Ike shook his head dumbly and couldn't think of a single thing to say. So he watched in silence as Annie carried the boy back up the steps and sat down on the front stoop beside him. Ike didn't know what she said to the boy to calm him down, but within a matter of minutes, the little guy was nodding and scrubbing a finger under his nose. Not long after that, he was smiling shyly again. Ike watched as Annie kissed the crown of his head with much gusto and hugged him close one final time. Then Mickey jumped up from the stoop and raced past Ike without looking at him, and joined the other kids in their completely disorganized and unorchestrated game of street hockey.

Annie, too, stood and ambled after him, stopping to pick up her duffel bag and toss it into the back seat. "I'm ready when you are," she said again as she opened the passenger side door and climbed inside.

Ike nodded and joined her in the car, then eased his way into the street at about a half a mile an hour to avoid the wildly scattering kids. When he braked for a stop sign at the corner, Annie looked over at him with a broad smile and asked, "If you could be any vegetable in the world, what would you be?"

As questions went, it wasn't one Ike heard often in his line of work. "I beg your pardon?"

"If you could be any vegetable in the world," she repeated, "what would you be?"

He turned right and headed toward the Schuylkill Expressway. "Why?"

Annie's smile broadened. "Because it occurs to me that we know absolutely nothing about each other, other than the fact that we were both gullible enough to be sucked into going to that bachelor auction. We've got a long drive to the shore ahead of us, so why not use the opportunity to find out a little bit more about each other, right?"

Sounded reasonable, Ike thought. But... vegetables?

"I'd be an eggplant, myself," she volunteered without being asked. "Eggplants seem to have it so together, don't you think? Not to mention having a sleek design and gorgeous coloring."

Ike drummed his fingers on the steering wheel and said nothing.

"Now you I see as more of a cauliflower kind of guy."

He flicked his right turn signal, veered onto the entrance ramp and melded smoothly with traffic before glancing over at Annie and repeating blandly, "Cauliflower."

She nodded. "Cauliflowers are pretty moody." She offered the observation as if that explained everything.

Ike sighed again, slipped on his Ray•Bans and settled back in the driver's seat. As Annie had just pointed out, it was going to be a long drive to the shore.

It was also, he admitted grudgingly some time later, a rather enjoyable drive, one that allowed him to discover a great many surprising things about his companion. In addition to wanting to be an eggplant, if Annie could be any fruit in the world, she wanted to be a kiwi. If given the choice of any animal in the world, she would be an ocelot. Any color, she would be green. Any musical instrument, she would be a banjo. Any supermarket product, a box of Velveeta. Any mode of transportation, a streetcar.

And so it had gone across the entire width of the great state of New Jersey. Whether he'd wanted to or not, Ike had learned more about Annie Malone than he had about any other human being he'd ever met. He knew she was thirty-two years old, a Virgo, and the youngest of two children. He knew she had two degrees in social work and one in child development, and that she had kicked the smoking habit three years ago, but still craved a cigarette now and then. On the few occasions when she indulged in alcohol, she *always* drank vodka martinis, very dry, no olive. She had gone to her senior prom stag and had received six stitches in her knee when she was seven years old.

Oh, yeah. And she was a widow.

That bit of information, when she'd offered it, had nearly sent Ike driving off the side of the road. She was too young to have experienced such a loss. Too fresh-looking. Too nice. She hadn't mentioned how her husband died, only that he had five years ago. And even having known her a short while, Ike could tell that Annie hadn't surrendered the information easily. Her husband's death was simply a part of her, like everything else she had told him, and therefore worthy of mention.

In turn, Ike had spoken little of himself, other than to oblige her with one- or two-word responses like "grapes," "wolf," "black," "tenor saxophone," "top sirloin" and "steam locomotive." He didn't like to talk about himself, preferred to keep private things private. He hadn't pried into Annie's life or asked many questions of her. She was just the type of person who revealed herself freely. Ike liked that about her. But it didn't mean he had to unburden himself in the process.

Now as he tossed his leather weekend bag on the bed in his room, he couldn't quite put thoughts of Annie to rest. She was, to say the least, an enigma. She was bright, attractive, and capable of doing just about anything she wanted to do. She smiled freely and spoke without inhibition. She was the kind of person one would expect to find living in sunshine and wide open spaces, amid nature's bounty, if not an actual part of it. Yet Annie Malone had buried herself in a decaying urban landscape, and had surrounded herself with damaged children who were the victims of life's darkest secrets.

It made no sense to Ike. He was the kind of man who put unpleasant thoughts as far from himself as he could. He'd had the most ordinary of upbringings and a very happy childhood—middle middle-class suburbs, public schools, a bicycle for Christmas when he was ten, twenty-five cents from the Tooth Fairy on a pretty regular basis, a craving for marshmallow cream on graham crackers that he'd never quite outgrown. He'd never had a reason or opportunity to suspect that other people had grown up any differently.

And although as an adult, he did know better, he still couldn't begin to understand the drive or motivation behind people who purposely put themselves into ugly situations when they didn't have to. Why would someone like Annie choose to live the way she did? What could she possibly be getting out of it?

Unable to answer the questions, he unzipped his bag and began to halfheartedly unpack. The early afternoon sun hung high in the sky, its rays tumbling through the open window to spill over the hardwood floor in streaks of white and gold. Across the street from the Hanson House Bed and Breakfast, the mighty Atlantic roared and crashed against the beach like a hungry beast. A warm breeze danced with the lacy curtains, redolent with the fresh scent of salt and the far-off fragrance of a barbecue grill warming up for lunch.

Ike paused in his activity to move to the window, inhaling deeply as he pushed it open more. He loved the ocean. Even with Craggedy Annie along for the ride—who was growing less craggedy, he had to confess—it was going to be nice to get away for the weekend. His work had become so demanding since he'd joined his company with his partner's some years ago. The merger had come at an ideal time and had suited well both men's needs. Ike had wanted more business, more opportunity. His partner, Chase Buchanan, had wanted more time to spend with his family. Both men had gotten exactly what they wanted from the deal, and the business had grown by leaps and bounds as a result.

Buchanan-Guthrie Designs, Inc. was now enormously successful, and Ike had more work than he had ever imagined he would. He ate, drank, breathed, slept . . . he absolutely *lived* his career, and liked it that way just fine. Working was what Ike did best. Maybe Chase was a family man, the perfect father. But Ike couldn't imagine living his life that way. He was too full of ambition to ever settle down. What would he do with kids?

Kids. He couldn't stop thinking about that kid.

That kid at Annie's. The one with the eyes so big and blue, they seemed to peer right into his soul. The one who had screamed in terror that Ike was going to hurt him. The one who had been so badly abused by his parents he didn't know any other way of being treated. Even a guy like Ike, who had no desire to have children, couldn't begin to understand how anyone could do that to a kid.

A soft rap on the door connecting his room to Annie's pulled him away from his thoughts, and back into his room. The Hanson House was a Victorian wonder, the owners clearly having cared for it as if it were a much-loved relative. Outside, the looming structure was trimmed in yellow and green, and it soared three stories high in a seemingly unplanned zigzag of angles and corners. Inside, the rooms were furnished with period pieces and accessories, painted soft colors suited to ocean living, and filled with sunlight. Ike and Annie had been placed in rooms on the third floor, rooms that had apparently been assigned to the servants way back when the Hanson House had been a private residence. And although his room was a bit small, the ceiling slanted on one side, it was cozy and welcoming and surprisingly accommodating.

"Nice place," Annie said when Ike opened the door. "Must be setting you back a bundle."

"Yeah, it is a nice place," he agreed, deciding it might be best to just avoid commenting on the second, more acerbic, half of her observation. "I guess Hanson House is a

world away from Homestead House, isn't it? Which re-
minds me," he added quickly when he saw her frown.
"Just exactly *what* is Homestead House, anyway?"

She rotated one shoulder in what he decided was a defensive gesture. "It's a house in town," she told him evenly.
"It's a place where people live. It's a home."

Ike nodded. "A home for unwanted kids, you mean."

Annie shook her head. "No, I mean it's a home. Period. Exactly like your place—whatever that place may
be—is a home." She straightened as she added, "And just
for the record, every one of those kids is wanted. Wanted
by me and my staff. They just have nowhere else to go for
the time being."

Ike eyed her thoughtfully. "You don't like me much, do
you?"

"No," she replied quickly, clearly not at all surprised by
the question or quick change of subject. "I don't."

"Why not?"

"Because you're the kind of person who's in the best
position to help other people, but you don't make a single
effort to do so."

"Because I have money?"

Annie shook her head again. "Not *because* you have
money, but because of the way you use it. And because you
have prestige and a position in the community you let go to
waste, too."

Ike took a step forward to lean against the doorjamb, a
gesture that brought him close enough to Annie to detect
just a hint of her perfume. It was a spicy scent, vaguely familiar. But he couldn't quite identify what it was. "What
do you mean?" he asked softly.

Relentlessly, Annie continued, "People like you run
around in an impressive social circle and have a lot of clout.
You have the ear of government officials, society leaders
and corporate bigwigs. You're high profile. You could do
a lot to improve the situation of other people who don't
have such opportunities. But the only benefits and profits

you reap from your status are strictly of a personal nature."

"Is that so?"

She nodded. "Yup."

"And that's why you don't like me."

"That's why I don't like you."

"Then I guess we're even," he muttered as he pushed himself away from the doorjamb again. "Because I don't like you, either."

His blunt statement appeared to surprise her, in spite of the fact that she'd spoken so frankly to him herself. "You don't?" Her voice was quiet and timid when she uttered the question, and she seemed to be genuinely distressed that he would find her unappealing. "Why not?"

"Because you're full of anger and resentment, you make snap judgments about people, and you're completely unrealistic. And dammit, Annie, nobody dresses the way you do nowadays. The Age of Aquarius ended twenty-five years ago. People found out they couldn't change the world with love-ins and protests. Nobody cared then. Nobody cares now. Deal with it."

He hadn't meant to go off like that, and, too late, Ike realized how awful he must have sounded. There was just something about Annie Malone that put him on edge and made him feel defensive. Something that made him quick to overreact. But before he could apologize and try to explain himself—no easy feat, since he didn't understand his behavior himself—Annie withdrew, both literally and figuratively.

She narrowed her eyes and clamped her mouth shut, then reached past Ike to curl her fingers over the doorknob, clearly intending to close the door tight, too. But she could only pull it closed a few inches before it hit his big body and stopped. Instead of moving away, he circled her wrist with loose fingers.

"I'm sorry," he said softly. "That was out of line."

"Yeah, it was," she agreed every bit as quietly. She glanced up and met his gaze, then looked past him into his room. "But you're right. I did make a snap judgment about you. And for that, I apologize, too."

Neither seemed to know what to say after that, and as much as Ike wished Annie would look into his eyes again, her gaze ricocheted everywhere but there. She did have nice eyes, he thought. Pale green irises ringed by a darker circle of color, and thick, dark lashes that were so perfect, they almost looked false. But if there was one thing Ike was certain about in Annie, it was that there was absolutely nothing false about her.

The silence between them stretched until it became even more uncomfortable than their angry exchange had been. Finally, he released her wrist and stepped away from the door. Without a word, she began to tug it toward herself again.

"I guess I'll just have to prove to you that you're wrong about me," he said when the door was nearly closed, wondering why it was so important that Annie Malone not misjudge him.

The door paused in its slow movement for only a moment, and he heard her reply softly, "I guess you will."

"How about grabbing some lunch?" he rushed on before she could close the door completely. "I know a great little place that most of the tourists overlook."

For one long moment, when she didn't reply right away, Ike thought Annie was going to tell him to take a flying leap. Not for the first time, he wondered why she had come along on this jaunt when she clearly would have preferred to be anywhere *but* alone with him in romantic surroundings. Then she surprised him by pushing the door open again.

She surveyed him slowly, literally from head to toe, then lifted her shoulders in a quick shrug. "Okay," she said. "I guess I am pretty hungry. And I wouldn't mind doing a little shopping. I promised the kids a couple of souvenirs. Just give me a few more minutes to get unpacked."

Ike nodded, oddly pleased to discover that he wouldn't be spending the entire weekend alone after all. He decided it might be best if he didn't think about how curious a realization that was when he'd awakened that morning wanting nothing more in the world than simply to be left alone. He hadn't wanted to leave Philadelphia, hadn't wanted to go anywhere with Annie Malone. But now that he was here in Cape May, alone with the woman he had been so sure would annoy him, he felt anything but annoyed.

What exactly he *was* feeling, he wasn't quite certain. But Annie's presence was doing something to him—something rather weird and wonderful—of that he was sure.

While he was mulling the revelation over, however, the door connecting his room to Annie's—and to her—closed with a quiet, but resolute, *click*.

Three

Ike needn't have worried that Annie would take his remark about her dressing habits to heart. When he knocked on her hotel room door some hours later—the real room to her door, not the connecting one—she responded to his summons wearing an ankle-skimming dress of some crinkly fabric, that buttoned from hem to scooped neck, claret in color and patterned with tiny flowers in pale yellow and ivory. A velvet, burgundy ribbon tied around her neck and simple gold hoops looped through her earlobes served as her only jewelry, and her hair hung down her back in a foot-long, loosely plaited braid. Her shoes were flat, the same texture and color as the ribbon around her neck, and as a result, she was forced to tip her head back substantially to meet his gaze.

She still looked like a hippie, he thought. But there was something about her getup that he found more than a little appealing.

And *Patchouli*, he suddenly realized. That was the scent that surrounded Annie Malone. But only faintly, as if it were the result of soap or powder, and not a heavily applied perfume. The fragrance was clean and fresh and slightly exotic, much like the woman herself. For some reason, Ike wanted to bend to bury his head in the curve of her neck and drink in great gulps of her scent. Only with a massive amount of restraint did he keep himself from doing just that.

"You look lovely," he said, surprising himself. He'd never called a woman *lovely* before. *Beautiful,* many times, *ravishing* on a few occasions, and *incredible* when the word seemed appropriate. But *lovely?* It was an outdated term, something a person normally used when referring to an elderly aunt. At least, that's what Ike had always thought before. But the word seemed somehow suited to Annie.

"Thanks," she said. She eyed his dove gray Hugo Boss suit, his pale lavender Geoffrey Beene dress shirt and his multihued pastel silk tie. Then she grinned mischievously. "You look like an ad for *GQ.*"

He narrowed his eyes at her tone of voice. "You don't make that sound like a compliment."

Her grin broadened, and her tone was playful as she assured him, "Oh, it wasn't meant to be."

He smiled back in spite of himself. "I see. You, no doubt, prefer a man in Levi's, Earth shoes and a Grateful Dead T-shirt, right?"

She lifted a hand to finger the necktie that was splashed with color like an abstract painting. She turned it over to check the label, smiled, then flattened her palm over the length of silk as she patted it back into place. "Hey, you're the one wearing the Jerry Garcia tie, Ike, not me."

It was the first time she had referred to him using his given name, and they both seemed to feel a little uncomfortable at having it hanging between them that way. Annie continued to meet his gaze levelly, tracing an idle pattern on his tie with her fingertip, seemingly oblivious to the oddly heated sensations her gesture raised elsewhere on his body. Before he became completely undone by the careless meanderings of her hand, Ike curled his fingers around hers and lifted her palm to his lips.

"You're right," he said after pressing his lips against the warm pad of her palm.

He had meant to say more, something about there being a little of the sixties in everyone, as hard as people like him tried to exorcise the decade. But the taste and feel of her skin on his seemed to numb his lips. Annie Malone may seem brittle and clipped, he thought, but she wasn't. She was soft. Warm. He didn't know how he could be so certain when he knew so little about her, but there were no edges to Annie, as much as she might try to make people believe that there were. And when Ike realized he was about to lift her hand to his mouth again for an even more intimate exploration, he quickly released her fingers and shoved his hands deep into his pockets.

"We'd better go," he said, hoping his voice sounded steadier than it felt. "Our reservation is for seven."

She nodded silently and preceded him down the hall. Ike followed closely behind, watching with much interest the way the skirt of her dress swung first one way and then the other in response to the subtle sway of her hips. He sighed. He had spent the entire afternoon following Annie all over Cape May in much the same way, wondering how he could have been so bothered by her hip-hugger jeans initially, when they hugged her hips so damned beautifully. The woman had some way of walking, he decided. And he couldn't help but be mesmerized by the way she moved.

Annie could feel his eyes on her as she made her way quietly down the stairs toward the first floor, just as she had felt his eyes on her all afternoon. For Pete's sake, what was he staring at? she wondered. He'd already gone out of his way to disparage her wardrobe, and she knew he didn't like the way she wore her hair. He quite clearly didn't like *her*, had even said so to her face. Although she loved the dress she was wearing, she knew it was old-fashioned and shapeless and revealed absolutely nothing of interest.

So, dammit, what was he staring at?

And what had that kiss on her palm been all about? She closed her eyes briefly as she remembered the rigidness of his torso beneath her hand when she'd straightened his necktie. She had always thought executives and businessmen were supposed to be flabby and soft. But Ike must get some kind of regular exercise, she thought, because he'd felt like solid rock beneath her fingers. Hot, solid rock, she realized further. Hot, solid rock that was alive and rabid and...

Stop it, she ordered herself when her thoughts started to become far too graphic. She was being silly. He was just some guy she was spending the weekend with. Some hot, rigid guy who—

Annie sighed fitfully and forced herself to pause at the foot of the stairs to let him catch up. She had no reason to be running away from him to begin with, she told herself. Just because he'd kissed her hand, and just because she'd felt that kiss wind a blazing trail all the way from her fingertips through her heart to her toes... Annie squeezed her eyes shut again and tried to remind herself that she didn't like Ike Guthrie. Unfortunately, that deep-seated animosity she had been so certain would be her constant companion this weekend had evidently packed up and gone home.

She made herself relax when he joined her at her side, inhaling a calming breath as he took her elbow lightly in his hand to lead her toward the dining room. The Hanson House was as renowned for its restaurant as it was for its hospitality, and Annie figured out why almost immediately. Even if they served nothing but greasy burgers and fries, people would keep coming back to this place. Because the dining room was so beautiful.

Where the bedrooms of the bed-and-breakfast were light and airy, the dining room was dark and intimate and cozy. A huge crystal chandelier hung at its center, dimmed low to mimic candlelight. Real candles flickered in crystal votives on each of the tables, all of which seemed to be isolated by virtue of very strategically placed potted ferns and lacy screens. The walls were papered in sapphire moiré, the mahogany chairs upholstered in gold velvet. The table to which the maître d' led them was draped with ivory lace, a single yellow rose rising from a crystal vase at its center.

"Wow, this place is wonderful," Annie said as she made herself comfortable. She tried not to notice how the candlelight flecked Ike's hair with bits of golden fire, tried to ignore the way his cheekbones appeared even more prominent in the shadows. Tried and failed miserably.

He picked up his menu and began to idly scan it. "Yes, it is. And I imagine it's a far cry from the way you usually have dinner."

Annie had picked up her menu and started to open it, but she slapped it shut and tossed it back onto the table when he uttered his comment. She wished he would quit making references to her life sound as if she were the little match girl. And she wished she would stop caring about what he thought of her.

"What's that supposed to mean?" she demanded.

He glanced up, clearly not understanding why she was angry. "What's what supposed to mean?"

"Why do you keep talking to me like I'm some indigent, ignorant rube?"

"I don't—"

"Yes, you do. Just about everything you've said to me since you picked me up this morning has been insulting. What I want to know is, why?"

He seemed genuinely surprised by her charge. "That's not true."

Annie lifted her hands, touching the index finger of one to the thumb of the other. "You've insulted my home," she began. She then pressed one index finger to the other. "You've insulted my neighborhood." She counted off the rest of her fingers as she added, "You've insulted the way I dress, my system of beliefs and my way of life." She dropped her hands to the table, folding them convulsively together to keep herself from popping him in the eye. "You've insulted *me*. Continuously. And I'm telling you to cut it out. Now."

He opened his mouth to argue, seemed to think better of it, and said simply, "Okay. I'm sorry. I didn't mean to. And it won't happen again."

Annie picked up her menu and studied the appetizers. "Thanks," she muttered.

They sat in uncomfortable silence for some moments, each seeming inordinately fascinated by their dinner choices. A wine steward came and went when Ike ordered something for them to drink that Annie had never heard of, then returned again with a bottle that was very dusty and old-looking. She watched Ike smile and nod his approval, then the steward opened the wine and poured a scant splash of red into Ike's glass. Annie studied him as he lifted the glass to his mouth and swallowed the contents, uttered a murmur of satisfaction and nodded again. The steward then filled Annie's glass before performing the same task for Ike's.

The whole episode lasted scarcely a minute, but Annie felt as if time had expanded to eternity. Her heart seemed to have climbed into her throat as she watched him sample the wine, and her stomach was still flip-flopping madly. Her breathing had become shallow and was making her feel faint. Her face and neck were hot, her hands sweaty. How could she possibly feel as if she'd just made love to the man when she'd done nothing but watch him take a sip of wine?

It was his mouth, she decided. Although Ike's chin and jaw were square and blunt, his cheeks rough with pale blond traces of a day-old beard, his lips were full and soft-looking. And without even realizing what was happening, she suddenly found herself indulging in a too realistic fantasy about what it would be like to feel those lips dragging openmouthed kisses along her calf and up the back of her thigh.

"Oh, jeez," she whispered, closing her eyes in an effort to dispel the image. But it remained firmly imprinted at the forefront of her brain.

"What?"

She heard Ike's roughly uttered question, but Annie kept her eyes closed for a moment longer, still unable to push the graphic fantasy away. When she finally did open them again, it was to find him staring at her in the oddest way. As if he wanted to yank her across the table and into his lap, hike up her skirt, and make love to her right there in front of everyone dining. That realization, of course, only agitated her further, and Annie struggled to regain control of her crazily spinning thoughts.

"I, um...I said, uh..." She knew her cheeks were burning bright red, and she snatched up her menu again. "'Jeez.' I said, 'Jeez.' As in, 'Jeez, look at all the dinner choices. How am I ever going to decide what to have?''

"That's not what you were thinking about."

She peeked over the top of the menu and saw that Ike still had that strange expression on his face. Only now his eyes were lit with laughter, and one corner of his mouth had lifted in just the slightest hint of a grin.

"I know *exactly* what you were thinking about just now," he said softly, setting his own menu aside. "I've seen that look often enough on a woman's face. You were thinking about having something all right, but it wasn't dinner."

Annie narrowed her eyes at him. "Boy, you have got some ego, you know that? As a matter of fact, food was exactly what I was thinking about. I was thinking that the breast...uh..." She felt herself coloring again and cursed her fair complexion.

The other corner of his mouth lifted. "What about the breast?"

"The breast of *chicken*," Annie said more forcefully. "I was thinking that the breast of chicken in Ike sauce...I mean *wine* sauce," she corrected herself hastily, "would be really good. For dinner."

Ike chuckled, a warm, pleasant eruption of laughter that sounded almost rusty from disuse. "I see," he told her, crossing his arms over his chest. "I can only imagine what you have in mind for dessert."

Annie made it a point to glance at the menu again, then without looking at him said, "Cheesecake."

"Funny, that's what I'm planning to have, too."

This time when she looked at him, the easy laughter was gone from his expression, replaced by a raw animal intent that she would have to be an idiot to mistake.

"Well, you'll have to get your own," she assured him faintly, hoping her voice didn't reflect the tremble that shook her as she uttered her statement. "Because I'm not sharing mine with you."

Ike said nothing, just continued to stare at her as if he knew for a fact that she would. Fortunately, their waiter arrived then to take their orders, and some of the sexual tension that was tying her in knots began to dissolve.

But it didn't go away completely.

She lifted her wine to her lips and filled her mouth with the ruby liquid, letting its buttery flavor warm and relax her all the way to her toes. All she had to do was get through this evening, she reminded herself. Tomorrow, right after lunch, they'd be returning to Philadelphia. In the light of day, she knew she could see Ike Guthrie for what he was and deal with him accordingly. But the darkness of night blurred his stark edges and blunted his angles. Something about the nighttime softened him, made him more approachable. All Annie had to do was make sure she didn't fall for the illusion. In the morning, things would be clear enough once more.

Unfortunately, she realized as she sipped her wine again, there were a good twelve hours between now and then. A lot could happen in twelve hours.

All she had to do was make sure nothing did.

Only ten hours to go, she thought as she glanced down at her watch while Ike signed their check. The two of them had managed to make it through dinner without any further little food-oriented double entendres, so the rest of the night should be a piece of cheesecake, right? Annie chided herself for the slip, and started to scoot her chair away from the table. Before she could do so, however, Ike was behind her, pulling her chair out for her.

She stood, cursing his height that made it necessary for her to tilt her head back so far to look at him. When she did, her braid fell away from her back, swinging like the end of a rope. "Thanks," she said.

Ike stared back down at her, catching her hair in his hand to still its back-and-forth motion. "Don't mention it," he told her as he pulled the long braid forward over her shoulder.

The back of his knuckles skimmed lightly over her skin just above her breast as he released her hair, and although she tried to give him the benefit of the doubt, Annie knew he had performed the gesture deliberately. She should have been offended, she told herself. Instead, for some reason, she felt oddly exhilarated.

"Let's take a walk," he suggested as he settled his hand at the small of her back, silently encouraging her to precede him. From behind her and near her ear, she heard him whisper further, "Along the beach. In the moonlight."

It was the last place on earth she knew she should go with Ike Guthrie. In spite of that, she found herself nodding in agreement as she walked beside him toward the door.

Late spring at the shore was perfect. No overriding heat, no suffocating humidity, no hoards of teenagers and tourists yet. The night was cool and breezy, and the beach was only sparsely populated by other couples like Annie and Ike. Except that most of those couples were probably involved in some kind of honest relationship that was really romantic, she thought, and not a blatant sham arranged through cajoling and bribery by their sisters.

Nevertheless, Annie felt relaxed and satisfied as she slipped off her shoes and wiggled her bare toes in the sand. And when Ike shrugged out of his jacket and tossed it casually over her shoulders, it seemed like the most natural thing in the world to snuggle more completely into the soft fabric made warm by and redolent of the man who was starting to drive her mad.

As she tucked her shoes into his jacket pockets and pulled the garment more closely around her, Ike strode leisurely and quietly beside her, his face profiled against the darkness by the faint lights of the hotels and restaurants across the street. The half moon hung high in the sky, cresting the gently swollen waves with bits of silver and pewter.

For a long time, the two of them walked along without speaking. Then Ike reached for Annie's hand and wove her fingers with his.

"How did your husband die?"

The question sliced through the silence and darkness like a knife, piercing her heart every bit as easily. "Why do you ask?"

He hesitated for a moment, then walked forward again. "I'm sorry. Just curious, I guess. I suppose it's really none of my business. But you're so young to have suffered a loss like that. What were you... twenty-seven when he died?"

She nodded.

"That's a lot to lose when you're that age."

"It's a lot to lose when you're any age," she corrected him.

"So, what happened?"

It really was none of his business, she thought. After tomorrow, she would never see him again, so what was the point in sharing life-changing revelations with the man? Still, it was no secret what had happened. There was nothing shameful or dishonest about Mark's death. And it was as much a part of Annie as Mark himself had been. Talking about it was no different than discussing her political opinions. Except for the fact that her political opinions didn't usually open up a big gaping hole in her soul.

She shrugged, deciding she might as well just tell Ike the unembellished version. "He was trying to intervene in a domestic dispute, and he was shot."

Ike stopped, then turned to face her completely. "What was he, a cop?"

"No, he was a social worker, like me. We founded and ran Homestead House together."

"So how did he wind up getting shot?"

Annie sighed and began to walk again, unable to remain still when the memories of that night crowded into her head. Ike let go of her hand and fell into step behind her, seeming to sense that she needed some space.

"One of our kids had been placed in a foster home," she began, "but not a very good one, I'm afraid. She called us one night when her foster parents were arguing. The husband was beating up the wife, and Lori was so terrified, she didn't know who else to call, so she called us. We called the police, but since the apartment was only a couple of blocks away, Mark took off, too, and got there before the cops did. When he tried to pull the guy off his wife, the guy turned around and shot him three times. One bullet severed his aorta. Mark died instantly."

It was amazing, Annie thought, how one could speak in such matter-of-fact terms about something that had shattered one's life. All the clichés about time had proved more or less true, and all things considered, she had healed fairly well. It had happened in small steps, with tiny victories. First, at some point, she had found the strength to get out of bed in the morning. Eventually, she had begun to eat again. Next, she had found it within herself to converse and share her grief with others. And after a while, she had managed to find a smile or two here and there.

Her kids had made all the difference. If it hadn't been for them, she may never have come back. But the children of Homestead House had depended on her. She'd had an obligation to them. And ultimately, they were the ones who'd been responsible for dragging her out of the dark hole into which she'd descended after her husband died. It was just one of the things that bound her to them so fiercely. Children had come and gone at Homestead since then, but Annie's relationship with them never changed. She needed them. They needed her. It was just that simple.

"I'm sorry, Annie." Ike's voice was strained and quiet and uncertain.

She shrugged and stared out at the dark ocean. "It was a long time ago," she said softly. "A lifetime ago."

She felt more than saw him move to stand beside her. "I'm still sorry. It shouldn't have happened to someone like you."

She reached for his hand again, and felt his palm press against hers immediately. "Thanks," she said.

He squeezed her hand gently and began to walk forward again. "I love nights like this," he said as he stared at the sky. "It's too bad we can't have spring all year long."

Annie was grateful for the change and blandness of subject, and knew instinctively that Ike's reason for the gesture was not because he was uncomfortable with the topic they'd been discussing, but because he wanted to free her from her troubling thoughts. Maybe he wasn't such a bad guy after all, she thought. And maybe, just maybe, the weekend wasn't going to be a total waste of time.

She inhaled deeply of the fresh air. "Yeah, it's nice to be someplace where you can really enjoy it, too." After a moment, she added, "So, what about you?"

He seemed startled by the question. "What about me?"

"Ever been married?" she clarified.

"Never."

"Ever come close?"

"Not even once."

"How come?"

That, too, seemed to stump him. "Isn't it obvious?"

She smiled. "What's obvious is that you're an intelligent, articulate man, who's relatively attractive—"

"*Relatively* attractive?"

"—and kind of enjoyable to talk to," she ended with a chuckle.

"*Kind of* enjoyable?"

"Well, let's not go overboard."

Ike chuckled, too. "I don't mind if you go overboard."

Annie smiled. Oh, what the hell. She might as well be truthful. "Okay, you're a gorgeous, nice guy who's successful and doesn't live at home with his mother. You're a good catch, Ike. So how come no woman has ever corralled you?''

He eyed her speculatively. But instead of answering her question, he replied, "Gorgeous? You think I'm gorgeous?''

"Don't tell me you're surprised.''

He nodded vehemently. "You bet I'm surprised. Not that I *am* gorgeous, mind you, just that you'd admit it.''

"Ike..."

He stopped walking again, looped his arms around her waist and hauled her against him. Before Annie knew what was happening, he bent his head to the curve of her shoulder and neck. He kissed her once, briefly, where her pulse jumped wildly against her throat. Then he straightened and met her gaze.

"I like the way you say my name," he told her. "Say it that way again."

Annie could scarcely remember her own name at that point, let alone the manner in which she'd spoken his. "What are you talking about?" she asked him on a ragged whisper. "How many ways can a person say your name? It's only three letters and one syllable. Ike. How can that—"

He interrupted her by bending to kiss her again, this time pressing his lips to hers in a kiss that was at once urgent and leisurely. He took his time to explore her mouth, but commanded a response from her to rival his own. Annie was helpless to do anything but kiss him back. Without thinking, she reached up to flatten her palms against his chest, feeling his jacket fall from her shoulders when she did so. As she clutched the soft fabric of his shirt in her fists, she met his demand with a fire to equal his own. His mouth was warm, damp and insistent, and she felt herself gradually drawn more fully into his embrace, closer, ever closer to him, until she nearly tumbled headfirst into his very soul.

She'd never been kissed like that before. Never. Mark had been much less—

Mark.

Her dead husband's face roared up into her brain then, and to her horror, Annie could scarcely remember what he looked like. She tore herself away from Ike and stumbled backward, nearly tripping over her own feet in the sand. She covered her mouth with one hand, her eyes with the other. Then she spun around and dropped both hands to her sides . . .

. . . and ran away as fast as she could.

Four

Ike stood for a long time in front of the door linking his room to Annie's, his palm pressed flat against the wood, fingers splayed, staring at it. She was still crying. He could hear her muffled sobbing as clearly as if she were in his room with him. He wished she was. Because if she was in his room with him, maybe then he could understand what it was that seemed to be eating her up inside. Maybe then he could apologize for kissing her so baldly on the beach. Maybe then he could figure out what he'd done to make her run away from him like that.

Maybe then he could kiss her again.

He lifted his other hand to knock, then dropped it to the doorknob instead. With one gentle turn to the left, the latch gave, and he pulled the door open toward him without a sound.

Annie lay on her bed facing him, her eyes wide open, holding a tissue beneath her nose. She was staring at him as if she'd been expecting him to come through that door, and without waiting to be invited or dismissed, Ike stepped into her room. The only illumination therein came from a standing lamp in the corner, a scant circle of hazy yellow that scarcely reached the room's center. She looked scared and vulnerable, and God help him, all he wanted to do was rush to her side and hold her.

Instead, he held himself firmly in place and asked, "Are you okay?"

She didn't reply one way or the other, only continued to lay on her side, staring at him. Then she sniffled, wiped her nose and blinked.

"Annie?" he tried again, taking a few experimental steps forward. "Are you okay?"

She pushed herself up on the bed and swung her bare feet to the floor. Her hair was falling out of her braid, and stray pieces hung in loose strands about her face. She'd removed her velvet ribbon and earrings, and the top few buttons of her dress were undone, revealing the little satin bow of the white undershirt she wore beneath.

"I'm fine," she said softly, tangling her fingers with the tissue and dropping her hands into her lap. "It's all right. I'm sorry." She finally glanced up at him, only to widen her eyes in dismay and look away again. "I'm fine," she repeated without much conviction.

Ike strode forward again, this time closing what little distance remained between them. He stood before her, towering over her, and curved his hand over the crown of her head to stroke his palm over her hair. He tried not to notice how silky it was, or how the soft tresses hanging loose about her face seemed to wrap themselves around his fingers of their own free will. Without even realizing what he was doing, he dropped his hand to her cheek, lightly tracing his thumb over her cheekbone and jaw before curling his index finger under her chin. When he tipped her head back to gaze fully upon her face, he saw that her eyes were wet and red-rimmed. She blinked, and a single fat tear tumbled down her face.

"You don't look fine," he said. "You don't sound fine, either. You want to talk?"

She pulled her head to the right, gently freeing herself from his touch. Her gaze fell to her lap, and she shook her head. "No. I'd rather not."

Ike dropped his hand helplessly back to his side. "Annie, I—"

He what? he wondered. He had no idea what to say to her at the moment. Finally, he just decided to tell her what he'd been thinking since she'd run away from him on the beach a short time ago.

"I'm sorry if I offended you when I kissed you," he said softly, curling his fingers behind her neck along her nape. For some reason, he simply couldn't tolerate not touching her. "But I won't apologize for doing it. And given the opportunity, I'd do it again in a heartbeat."

"You didn't..." Her head snapped back up, and her eyes met his levelly in the soft light. But she didn't pull away from him this time. "It wasn't the kiss that upset me," she whispered.

His fingers wandered into her hair again, marvelling at how the sandy-colored tresses caught what little light was available in the room and tossed it back like a beacon. "Then what's wrong?"

She hesitated, keeping her gaze steadily trained to his. "It was the way..." She sighed heavily. "It was the way you made me feel."

Ike moved to sit beside her on the bed, the old mattress creaking and groaning at the added weight when he did so. Surely this wasn't a good idea, he told himself as he draped his arm over her shoulder. Surely what he was doing was just about the stupidest thing in the world he could do. Sitting on a bed, in a very romantic inn, with a woman who was turning him inside out, whom he'd kissed and made run away. No, not the smartest thing he'd ever done before.

Nevertheless, he heard himself ask her, "How did I make you feel?"

It was a long time before she answered him. She didn't move, didn't speak, didn't even seem to breathe. She only sat for several moments in silence, as if she were thinking about something, something she didn't want to consider.

Finally, she told him, "You made me feel like...like I was alive again. For the first time since Mark was killed, I felt myself come alive inside. Until you...until you kissed me, I hadn't realized how numb I had become, how much of myself I had let die with Mark. And now..."

Her voice trailed off, but she continued to watch him closely, as if she were scared of what his reaction to her revelation would be.

And his reaction was pretty scary. It wasn't what she had said that made Ike flinch. It was what she didn't say. Annie Malone was telling him she hadn't been with anyone since her husband. That she'd been alone and unsatisfied ever since her husband's death. That it had been five years since a man, any man, had made her feel like a woman. Five years.

Five years.

"And you made me feel..." She hesitated again, as if she were now thinking about something that made her feel guilty. "Different," she finally concluded. "You made me feel different."

"Different from what?" he wanted to know. "Different how?"

Once again she dropped her gaze to the fingers in her lap that were turning the crumpled tissue into a wad of shredded lint. "I'd rather not talk about it," she said softly.

He nodded. "Okay. Then let me talk instead."

She glanced up again and opened her mouth to stop him, so he hurried on before she could interrupt.

"You make me feel strangely, too, Annie. I was dreading this weekend more than you could possibly know. I only went along with that stupid bachelor auction because my sister has always been able to talk me into doing things I wouldn't normally do. I was afraid I was going to wind up purchased by some greedy, simpering, superficial jerk, and that I'd be saddled with her for an entire evening. And at the time, I could think of no greater torture than that."

The arm he had draped over her shoulder moved lower, circling her waist, and Ike pulled her closer to himself. "But now I think I *can* imagine a greater torture. It's being saddled with you instead, and for an entire weekend at that."

When her expression of confusion turned to one of outrage instead, he smiled. "Not because you're greedy and simpering and superficial. Or boring and bland for that matter, as I originally thought you were going to be." His smile faltered as he clarified, "But because ever since we arrived in Cape May, all I've been able to do is try to come up with some way to convince you to let me spend the night in your bed instead of my own."

"Ike..." she began. But she left unsaid any objection she had been about to utter. Instead, she simply stared at him, studying his face as if she were trying to find the answer to some very important question.

He lifted his free hand to her hair, winding a stray piece around his index finger. "Earlier this evening," he continued, "all I wanted was to make love to you tonight and be on my merry way tomorrow."

"And now?" she encouraged him. "What is it you want now?"

Because he could no longer stand being this close to her without kissing her, Ike bent and pressed his lips to her cheek in the most chaste way he could manage. Then he tipped his forehead to hers. "That's where the torture part comes in. I still want to make love to you tonight. Badly. But I don't want be on my merry way tomorrow."

"Oh, Ike..."

"And it's beginning to tear me up inside, this wanting you, knowing you don't want me."

She hesitated only a moment before she admitted quietly, "I never said I didn't want you."

It was all the encouragement he needed. He bent to kiss her again, opening his mouth over hers as he urged her backward onto the bed. When she lay beneath him, his hand fell to her waist, flattening against her abdomen before skimming higher to slide between her dress and undershirt, completely covering her breast. Annie groaned when he closed his hand over the small, warm mound of flesh, palming it to life. When she did, he slipped his tongue into her mouth, savoring her sweetness with every stroke. She splayed her hands open over his chest, then dragged one lightly over his shoulder and along his neck to tangle her fingers in his hair. Cradling his head in her hand, she explored his mouth with a fierceness to rival his own.

The fragrance of her enveloped him, until he felt himself growing dizzy. He dropped his hand to the hem of her dress, tugging the soft cotton up along her bare leg, over her calf and higher, until he could cup the warm flesh of her thigh in his hand. His fingers found the fabric of her panties and dipped below it, curving into her soft derriere and pulling her closer to him. He felt her warmth collide with the thickening ridge at the apex of his own thighs, and he rubbed himself languidly against her. Annie groaned again, dropping her hand to his buttock, pulling him closer to herself still. Again, she kissed him, trailing a series of hot, damp kisses along his neck and throat.

For one brief, blissful moment, Ike thought the two of them were about to embark on a journey neither was likely to forget. Then Annie tore her lips from his neck, disentangled their bodies, and leapt up from the bed. She crossed her arms over her chest, her breath came in uneven gasps, her back was ramrod-straight, and she didn't look at him. Ike rolled to his stomach on her bed, tried to control his own ragged respiration, willed his too wound up body to calm down, and wondered what had just gone wrong.

"Annie—" he began.

"But wanting you doesn't mean I can have you," she interrupted him softly. "Wanting is ... It's ..." She shook her head slowly without completing the statement.

With some difficulty, Ike jackknifed into a sitting position, settled his elbows on his knees and dropped his head into his hands. "Why can't you have me?" he asked her without looking at her. He tried to lighten the mood some by reminding her, "You own me for the weekend, remember? I'm bought and paid for."

Unfortunately, Annie didn't seem to want light. Without looking at him, she said softly, "But I didn't buy you. I didn't pay for you. My sister did. She's the one who owns you. You're just a loaner."

"Then how about taking me because I'm willing to give myself to you?" he suggested further, now completely serious. When she didn't respond, he lifted his head to look at her and found that she still hadn't changed her position.

"Annie?" he said.

Finally, she turned to study him in the faint light. "Because I'm not willing to take you."

"Why not?"

"Because it wouldn't be right."

"It would be more than right. It would be—"

She turned her back on him again and dropped her gaze to the floor. "I think you'd better go."

Ike hesitated before speaking again, wondering if he was just asking for trouble by voicing what he suspected was the truth. "It's your husband, isn't it?"

When she whirled around like a cyclone to glare at him, he knew he had his answer.

"My husband has nothing to do with this," she insisted. "And he sure as hell isn't any of your business."

"I think your husband has everything to do with this," he countered. "And he became my business the minute you told me about him."

"You're wrong. Mark has—"

"Mark's gone," Ike interrupted gently. "He's been gone for five years. You're not being unfaithful to him by responding to another man. It's perfectly natural for you to—"

She held up a hand to halt anything more he might have to say. "You have no idea what you're talking about," she told him. "How could you? You've never been married."

He expelled a restless breath. "No, I haven't."

"Have you ever even been in love?"

"No."

"Then you can't possibly understand."

Ike stood and crossed to stand before her, cupping his palm under her chin. She resisted at first when he tried to tilt her head back so that he could meet her gaze, but finally looked up at him. He noticed then that her eyes weren't entirely green. A soft circle of amber surrounded her pupil. Somehow, the contrast in color made her eyes appear deeper, more expressive, more agonized.

"What I understand," he said, "is that, regardless of anything else you might say or feel, you respond to me in a way that's spontaneous, earthy and hot."

Two bright spots of color flashed in her cheeks at his roughly uttered statement, and her eyes seemed to darken in anger.

"You can deny it all you want," he told her, "but you'll never make me believe that you don't want something to happen between us as much as I do."

"You're wrong. I—"

"Never," he repeated. "I can *feel* it, Annie. Just now, I could *feel* how much you wanted to go through with what we were about to do. The only reason you pulled back is because you think you're betraying your husband. Or at least, your husband's memory. It's true, isn't it? You know it is."

"What I know..." Her breathing came in deep, uneven sputters, and her hands closed into fists. "What I know is that you couldn't possibly understand. No one could. Not unless they've been through it."

"He's dead, Annie. And you're alive. You're young, you're human and you have needs and desires that you've been neglecting. Your husband wouldn't expect or want you to die along with him."

For a long moment, neither of them said anything more. The silence in the room seemed to increase until it was nearly intolerable. Annie was the first to look away.

"I think you better go," she said again.

Reluctantly, Ike nodded, knowing it would be pointless to argue with her. She was right in one respect. He didn't for a moment understand her reasoning for retreating from him the way she had. But he figured she'd probably done the right thing. For now. He supposed he should be grateful one of them had managed to scrape up enough sense to retreat. Because he'd never had such an explosive reaction to a woman before.

If he was honest with himself, he had to admit that he was every bit as confused as she by the sudden turn of events. Only hours ago, the two of them had been standing toe-to-toe, each assuring the other of a mutual and very profound dislike. Now here they were, on the verge of indulging in an act traditionally reserved only for those who were deeply in love.

It didn't make sense. And maybe that was what Annie had meant when she'd said it wouldn't be right. Or maybe she'd meant something else entirely. At this point, Ike was so confused, he didn't quite know what to think.

"I'll go," he told her as he turned away. "But I'm not going far."

He paused as he strode past her, settling a hand firmly on her shoulder. "You won't get rid of me that easily," he assured her before he moved on again.

He kept moving until he was in his own room, and without speaking or turning around, he pushed the door closed behind himself. He didn't want to see the expression on Annie's face. He didn't want to see how she looked when she was sending him away.

With any luck at all, he thought as he undressed for bed, he'd never have to see her look like that again. With any luck at all, the next time he saw Annie, when he knocked on her door the following morning, she'd be welcoming him with open arms.

Annie stared at the door as it closed softly behind Ike. This wasn't how it was supposed to be happening, she thought. This wasn't what she'd had in mind for the weekend at all. She was supposed to have muddled through it with little or no problem, was supposed to have tolerated the presence of the big blond man who'd meant nothing to her only twenty-four hours ago, and then she was supposed to have gone back to her life in Philadelphia none the worse for wear. She had planned to wake up Monday morning with a much fatter bank account for Homestead House and without further thought or care for Ike Guthrie.

Her gaze wandered to the clock on the nightstand, and she saw that it was just past 2:00 a.m. She told herself that, technically, it was morning. Technically, there were fewer hours between now and sunup than had passed since sundown the day before. Technically, she had spent the night in Cape May with the man her sister had purchased for her. And, technically, she had upheld her end of the bargain. Now she could go home.

She could still wake up in good conscience Monday morning with a much fatter bank account for Homestead House. However, her conscience where Ike Guthrie was concerned wouldn't be nearly so cooperative. Annie was going to be plagued by thoughts of him for a long, long time. And she was going to care.

She recalled again the way she had felt when he'd kissed her on the beach. She'd been surprised by the immediacy and intensity of her reaction to him. She'd been amazed at how fully and readily her libido had jarred to life, as if it hadn't lain dormant for years.

And she recalled the way she had reacted to him later, in her room. The way her stomach had caught fire when he had dragged his fingers along the length of her bare leg. The way her breathing had become shallow when he'd cupped her breast firmly in his hand. The way her insides had melted at the pressure of his ripening arousal rubbing against her. She remembered in minute detail the way he'd sounded, smelled, tasted....

She squeezed her eyes shut, fighting back new tears. She tried to remember the way Mark had made her feel. Tried to recall if she'd experienced the same mind-scrambling sensations when her husband had made love to her. But to her great dismay, all she could recall was a pleasant, satisfying, warm, rosy joining. She didn't think she'd ever felt herself coming apart at the seams when her husband had made love to her so many years ago. There hadn't been the urgency, the demand, the *need* that Ike made her feel.

She told herself it was because what she'd shared with her husband had been noble and loving, and had gone much, much deeper than simple carnal lust. Ike Guthrie spoke to her body, not to her heart nor to her mind. And it was only her body that was replying to that summons. What she felt for him was nothing more than a physical reaction, a perfectly normal response under the circumstances. Human beings were sexual animals. It was something she'd learned in Psych 101. Annie just happened to be an animal who hadn't had sex for a very long time. Her body, too long without the natural satisfaction it craved, was responding to a sexual stimulus, she told herself. That was all Ike Guthrie was.

But what a sexy stimulus.

Again, involuntarily, she replayed every moment of their recent encounter, reliving once more each tender touch, each commanding caress. She supposed it would be a long time before she would be able to banish the memory completely. Perhaps she never would.

"Which is all the more reason you have to get out of here," Annie whispered to herself. One memory like that plaguing her was bad enough. She wasn't sure she'd be able to cope with what would happen the next time Ike came near her.

Without further thought or self-analysis, she pulled her duffel from beneath the bed and began to stow her belongings back inside. She shed her dress and donned jeans and a sweater, then reached for the phone and punched the number that would connect her to the front desk. It rang three times before a young-sounding voice answered.

"This is Annie Malone in room thirteen," she said. "I'm going to need to know when the first train leaves for Philadelphia, and I'm going to need a taxi to take me to the station."

Ike sat at his desk in his high-rise Philadelphia office and stared out the window at the quickly darkening sky. The red stain of sundown provided a stark backdrop for the towering dark skyscrapers, their windows patches of white that gradually winked off one by one. As usual, he was working late. As usual, his light would be one of the last to be extinguished. As usual, he was reluctant to go home. Because all he'd do once he got there was microwave some single-serving something from the freezer, eat it without tasting it as he leaned against the kitchen counter, then make himself comfortable in bed with nothing but the *Inquirer* to keep him warm.

As usual, he was thinking about Annie Malone.

It had been more than two weeks since he'd made the long drive from Cape May back to Philadelphia alone. He had to admit now that when he'd knocked on the door connecting his room to Annie's the day after their ill-fated brush with intimacy, he hadn't been much surprised to find her gone. And when the desk clerk had confirmed that for him, had told him that Ms. Malone had come down to the lobby before dawn to meet a taxi she had requested to take her to the train station, Ike had pretty much felt reassured of something he'd already guessed.

It wasn't that Annie didn't want him. She'd admitted herself that she did. It wasn't that she couldn't have him. He'd offered himself to her, no strings attached. And it wasn't that she didn't know what to do with him. He recalled himself that Annie had known *exactly* what went on between a man and a woman. No, what he'd guessed about Annie Malone—and what he now knew to be true—was that she was scared. Scared of him and of herself. Scared of what the two of them had somehow generated together.

Ike loosened his tie and leaned back in his chair, ignoring the blueprints on his desk that demanded his attention, and wondering instead about the mess he'd managed to tangle himself up in. Why, of all women, did it have to be Annie Malone? Why did she set his mind to reeling when other women only mildly interested him? And what was he going to do about it now?

He should just forget about her, he told himself. It wasn't as if he were hard up for feminine companionship. There were plenty of women far more glamorous and interesting—and far more interested in him, he thought with a frown—than Annie Malone. Women who would be more than happy to go out with him, and who wouldn't make him feel guilty for being the kind of man he was, or for living the way he did.

Women who wouldn't push him away just when things were starting to heat up nicely.

Problem was, Ike didn't think about those women anymore. He couldn't, because his brain was too full of memories about Annie Malone. Dammit.

He rose and rounded his desk, moving to stand in front of the fifteen-foot high, floor-to-ceiling windows that showcased the city in panorama. In darkness, with the glitter of lights, standing high above it and looking down as he was, the place almost looked beautiful. But as was the case with most big cities, Philadelphia could be a mean, frightening, dangerous place, especially at night. And Annie was out there somewhere, he thought. Out there all alone.

He looked to the west, where her crumbling neighborhood was probably just starting to come alive for the night. Alive with thieves and pimps and prostitutes, with gangs and drug dealers and killers. It was no place for Annie. And it was certainly no place for her children. What the hell was she doing, living there, in a house that was on its last legs, probably just barely squeaking by code?

A hammer and a few nails and a couple of gallons of paint would go a long way toward making it more of a home, he thought. Of course, it would still be in that lousy neighborhood. But at least it wouldn't look so depressing.

Ike moved away from the windows and returned to his seat, switching on the desk lamp to illuminate the blueprints before him a little better. He'd be working even later than usual tonight. Because other than the new beautification project for the city that he and Chase would be starting in a couple of weeks, this was the only pressing project on his docket right now. When it was done, he could take a few days off. His partner wouldn't mind. Hell, Chase was always telling Ike he worked too hard anyway. It was a funny sentiment coming from a man who, until a few years ago, had been exactly the same way.

Then Ike thought about Chase's wife, Sylvie, and the two little blond-headed girls who invaded the office to visit their father more often than Ike had ever approved. He smiled a little absently now. Maybe Chase's admonishments about Ike's workaholic tendencies weren't so incomprehensible after all.

He studied the blueprints on his desk, plans for a rambling, ultramodern CEO's mansion in Bucks County complete with swimming pool, tennis courts, and riding stables. But what he saw instead was a cramped, disintegrating, inner-city brownstone with virtually no yard at all.

Yeah, a little paint and a bit of renovation would make a big difference in Annie's house. He didn't think she'd mind. It would be good for her kids, after all. But best of all, Ike thought as he absently doodled Annie's name on the blueprints, he knew somebody who could do the work cheap.

Five

When Ike pulled his car to the curb in front of Annie's house two days later—his old battered Jeep this time, not the Lamborghini—the big brick building was every bit as decaying and ugly as it had been three weeks before. He marveled again that a woman like her could call such a place home. When he approached the front door, he prepared himself for an attack of children like the one that had assailed him the last time he had visited. But this time Annie's house was quiet.

Until he knocked on the front door.

Nearly a dozen people answered his summons. Leading the crowd was the curious little boy he had met before, Mickey, he recalled now. Rushing up behind him were assorted and sundry characters of all ages, sizes and colors, and bringing up the rear, looking at Ike as if she'd never met him before, was Annie.

She was dressed in blue jeans and an oversize, tie-dyed T-shirt, a kaleidoscope of reds and yellows. Her hair hung loose down her back and over her shoulders, and her face was washed clean of makeup. She was, he realized much to his dismay, more beautiful than he remembered. He opened his mouth to greet her, but was halted by someone else's words.

"Hi," Mickey said as he reached up to unlock the security door. He pushed it open with both hands and grinned.

Ike couldn't help but grin back. The little guy was missing two front teeth, leaving an oddly appealing, rectangular-shaped gap at the center of his smile.

"Annie," the little boy added as he looked over his shoulder at the woman in question, "you were wrong. He did, too, come back. I told you so."

Ike arched a brow in query at Annie, only to see her blush furiously and turn her attention to the others.

"Okay, everybody," she said, pushing her way through the kids and gently disbursing them. "Excitement's over. You've seen who our visitor is, and now that you know it's no one, you can go back to what you were doing."

When the sea of children finally parted—loudly and boisterously and raucously—and Ike stood face-to-face with her, he repeated, "No one? I'm no one?"

Her blush intensified. "You know what I mean."

"No, I don't. Please, explain it to me."

Annie opened her mouth to do just that, then closed it again when she realized she couldn't. Ike Guthrie certainly wasn't *no one*. She knew that for a fact, because *no one* wouldn't have been such a big *someone* in her thoughts lately. And in her memories. And her dreams. Oh, boy, had Ike been someone in her dreams recently, she remembered, feeling an odd heat wind from her stomach to her heart to some other parts of her she'd rather not have feeling hot right now.

"Umm..." she began.

"Well?"

Helplessly, she let her gaze consume him, from the white-blond hair that was wind-tossed and silky-looking, lingering a moment longer than necessary at his eyes before moving downward over his blunt, unshaven jaw, and the

strong column of throat. His skintight T-shirt had faded
from what had probably once been navy into patchy bits of
a dozen shades of blue. Her gaze slowed as she considered
the way the soft fabric strained at the sleeves over salient
biceps, and conformed lovingly to every bump and bunch
of muscle on his torso. Then her gaze dropped lower, halt-
ing at the waistband of his jeans, jeans that seemed to be a
million years old, so pale was their color, the fabric thin
enough to outline what she already knew to be a very. . .
prominent . . . attribute.

As if her dreams hadn't been troubling enough lately.

Annie snapped her eyes shut and blushed even more.
Then she heard Ike chuckling, and she reluctantly opened
them again.

"Okay, so I'm not no one," he said with a smile, clearly
understanding just how thoroughly she had been ogling
him, seeming to enjoy having the tables turned on him in
such a way. Before she realized what he intended to do, he
bent and kissed her quickly on the mouth, then straightened. "I missed you, too," he added softly.

Annie had automatically tipped her head back to facili-
tate his kiss, and had helplessly closed her eyes in anticipation. When he pulled away, she continued to hold the
position, not realizing that she even did so. Not until he
bent and kissed her again. Harder this time. With much
more feeling. His lips against hers were warm and damp,
coaxing a response she was helpless to deny him. He kissed
her the way a man kisses a woman when he's been away for
too long. He kissed her as if he cared for her.

And that was when Annie pulled away.

"Umm," she began again. She stepped back and
scrubbed a hand over her face, and tried to pretend the last
several moments had never occurred. "Uh, that is . . . what
are you doing here?"

He held up a brown paper bag and extended it toward
her. As she unfolded the flap on it, her told her, "Yester-
day, I went to put on my suit that I wore that night in Cap

May, and, along with a lot of sand, I found one of those in each pocket of my jacket.''

Annie peeked into the bag and saw her burgundy velvet shoes. She'd missed them when she'd unpacked her duffel upon her return to Philadelphia, but she hadn't yet managed to work up the nerve to call Ike and ask for their return. She hardly ever went anywhere that she needed to dress up, she'd told herself. Maybe someday, if she ever had cause to wear the shoes again, *then* she'd call Ike about them. By then, she'd thought, she probably wouldn't be so worked up over him anymore.

Yeah, right, a little voice inside her head piped up.

''Thanks,'' she told Ike before the little voice could say anything more. She took a step toward the front door and started to open it. ''It was nice of you to bring them all this way. You really didn't have to. You could have mailed them.'' She was babbling and she knew it, but she couldn't think of anything that would end the conversation effectively. Finally, she just pushed the front door open wide, thanked him again and concluded with, ''Goodbye.''

But Ike didn't take the hint. He *understood* the hint, she decided when his eyes sparkled with laughter. He just didn't *take* it.

''Actually, there was another reason I stopped by,'' he confessed.

Annie arched her eyebrows, though whether the gesture was the result of curiosity or anxiety, she wasn't certain. She closed the front door and took a step back. ''Oh? And what was that?''

Wordlessly, he indicated the other item he'd brought with him, a big, boxy hunk of metal with peeling red paint, held in his grip at knee-height, which was why Annie hadn't noticed it before. Her inventory of Ike hadn't gotten much below his waist. Just low enough to make her feel a little...crazy.

''It's a toolbox,'' she stated unnecessarily, still puzzled.

Ike nodded. ''Yes, it is. And you win the prize for guessing correctly.''

"What's the prize?"

He grinned. She found herself hoping his answer would be *Me,* but he said instead, "A complete home renovation performed by yours truly."

She shook her head slowly. "But I don't need a complete home renovation."

He dispelled a rude sound of concurrence. "You're right. What you need is a completely new home. You really ought to move out of this place, Annie. Not only is it an eyesore that could collapse on you any day now, but in case you haven't noticed, this is kind of a dangerous neighborhood."

She frowned at him. So they were back to that, were they? "Look, I already told you—"

"I know," he interrupted her. "And I'm not criticizing. I'm stating a fact. Annie, this isn't the place for kids. Or you. It's dangerous."

She sighed fitfully. She knew that. She knew Homestead House was in a bad neighborhood. She knew it was exactly the kind of neighborhood most of the kids had grown up in, which was part of their problem. She knew she should get them as far away from their urban existence as possible. But that took money. Money she didn't have and couldn't seem to get anyone interested in contributing to her, no matter how hard she tried to solicit donations.

"It's all I have," she told Ike simply. "It's all any of us here has right now."

He nodded. "Then let me help you fix it up some. I'm good at this kind of thing, honest. And I won't charge you a dime."

"Why?"

He looked at her as if she should already know the answer to that question, but Annie, being a realist, couldn't imagine why anyone like Ike would do anything for anyone like her, unless there was something in it for him. So she stared right back at him, silently demanding an answer to her question.

"Because I like you," he told her.

It wasn't exactly what she had expected to hear, but for some reason, she felt certain what he said was the truth. And after the way she'd abandoned him without a word three weeks before, she couldn't imagine why the man would want to do anything nice for her at all. Nevertheless, Annie knew he was right about the house. It did need a lot of work. She had planned to use part of her sister's donation—she still had to force herself not to call it "sucker money"—to have the most urgent repairs made. But if Ike was offering to perform them at no charge, why should she refuse?

Well, there was the small matter of having him in her home, she thought. Having him in her home meant having him close to her. And having him close to her meant she would continue to feel all the confusing, disquieting things she'd been feeling since that night in Cape May. She would find herself reliving that night over and over and over. And she would keep on feeling guilty. Feeling like a traitor to her husband's memory. Ike's presence in her home would quite possibly make her go mad.

"Uh, I'm not sure it's a good idea," she told him reluctantly.

He smiled. "What's not a good idea? Liking you or fixing up your house?"

"Yes, that."

"Which?"

"The house fixing part."

"So it *is* a good idea for me to like you."

"No, I meant . . ." She sighed fitfully and shifted her weight from one foot to the other. Ike's presence in her home was already making her go mad. What was the question again? she wondered.

"Of course it's a good idea," he told her, and she still didn't know exactly what they were talking about.

"But you have a business to run," she reminded him. "How can you possibly have time—"

"It's Saturday. I have the weekends to myself. Even *I* don't work that hard."

"But—"

"And I've given myself next week off." He smiled. "I can do that, you know. I'm the boss. And I need a vacation."

"Then go to the shore," she told him, hating the clipped, desperate tone of voice she couldn't mask.

He shook his head. "Nah. The last time I went to the shore, the weekend wound up being in no way relaxing."

Annie had the decency to feel embarrassed. "All right," she finally conceded. "But if you won't take money in return, then I'll think of some other way to repay you. I don't know how, yet, but I owe you, Ike. I owe you a lot."

"Oh, don't worry, Annie," he said with a big, salacious smile. "I'm sure I can come up with one or two ways to collect repayment. Just give me a little time."

She supposed she'd set herself up for that, she thought as he continued to gaze at her with a sexual implication he didn't even try to hide. But that didn't mean she had to go along with him and carry it any further. As much as she might want to.

"Fine," she said noncommittally. "Where do you want to start?"

Ike shook his head slowly, clearly disappointed that she was unwilling to play games with him. "Might as well start in the basement," he said. "The most enduring structures start with a solid foundation that needs to be continuously reinforced."

It was a perfectly logical statement coming from an architect in reference to a building, Annie thought. So how come Ike seemed to be speaking simply as a man, and about something other than a dilapidated row house?

Because you haven't been getting enough sleep lately, that irritating voice piped up again. *And why haven't you been getting enough sleep lately? Because you've been having all those wicked, graphic dreams about the man who's come to invade your house.*

Annie sighed, told the little voice to please shut up and mind its own business, and wondered how long Ike would be staying.

"What's that?"

Ike drummed his fingers on the length of dripping, rusty pipe over his head and tried not to feel impatient. *What's that?* had become a phrase that threatened to send him into a paroxysm of exasperation, so frequently had he had to answer the question lately. He turned to look at the little boy who had been uttering the query about every thirty seconds since he'd joined Ike in the basement two hours ago.

Mickey Reeser was a confoundingly cute kid. He was also annoying as hell. Nonetheless, Ike was surprised to discover that he liked the little guy. In spite of his experiences, Mickey could laugh and smile and be inquisitive, just like a six-year-old boy should. Although there was an undeniable hesitancy and uncertainty about his actions, the boy was getting on with his life. The kid was a survivor. Ike couldn't help but respect that. He just wished Mickey didn't ask so many damned questions.

"It's a pipe wrench," he said in response to the latest.

Before Mickey could ask the question Ike knew was coming next, he handed over the tool in question for the boy's inspection. *What's that?* was rivaled only by *Can I see it?* when it came to phrases that drove Ike nuts.

Mickey turned the heavy wrench over and over in his hands, running his fingers along the length of it several times before he gave it back to Ike. With mumbled thanks, Ike went back to work on the pipe above his head, wondering for perhaps the hundredth time since that morning what on earth he thought he was doing here in Annie's house.

He hadn't even guessed at the wretched state of the place until he'd gotten a closer look. The basement alone was a good nominee for Decay of the Decade. In the stark white light of the bare bulb swinging overhead, Ike could see a dozen cracks in the walls where water was gradually seeping in. The concrete floor was cracked, too, even crumbling in spots. Above him, the water pipes were more rust than metal, and the wood flooring above that was showing definite signs of the onset of water rot.

Ike sighed. He supposed he should be grateful he hadn't come across any evidence of rats. That hadn't much helped him deal with the big crickets and cockroaches, however. He shuddered. God, he hated bugs. Especially big bugs.

The jangle of metal against metal caught Ike's attention, and he turned to find Mickey sorting idly through his toolbox. He was about to tell the boy to knock it off, because he took great care in keeping his tools in order and didn't want to have to go to the trouble of reorganizing them before he left. Then he remembered the kid's expression a few weeks ago when he'd set off the alarm on Ike's car. He didn't want to ever see a child looking that frightened again. There was nothing in the toolbox that was dangerous, he reminded himself. Hell, what difference did it make if the kid mixed everything up?

"Be careful," he said halfheartedly. "Some of those things are pretty heavy."

"I can handle it," the little boy assured him.

As if to illustrate just the opposite, he dragged a huge, heavy flashlight out of the box and promptly dropped it on the floor. The impact with the concrete shattered the light's glass lens, and, just as Ike feared, the boy flinched and gazed over at him in terror.

"I...I...I...I'm sorry," he stammered, his voice hoarse with fear. "I didn't mean to, honest. I'm sorry. I...I...I..."

Ike started to approach him, then stopped when Mickey scrunched up his body and covered his head with his hands. Involuntarily, Ike clenched his own hands into fists. No child should be that scared of anything, he thought. He wished he could have five minutes alone with the little boy's parents. Nothing would bring him greater pleasure at the moment than teaching *them* a thing or two about fear.

"Mickey, it's okay," he said as softly as he could. "It was only a flashlight, and I can get another one on the way home today. Just be careful of the broken glass. I don't want you to hurt yourself."

Mickey stayed tightly rolled up in a ball, but he didn't cry or scream as Ike had feared he might. He took a couple of experimental steps forward, finding some comfort in the fact that the boy didn't grow more terrified. But he still didn't uncoil from his position of self-preservation. Before he could stop it, an image flared up in Ike's mind, one of a boy that small curled up into an ineffectual ball as he tried to fend off the blows of a much larger, full-grown man. This time Ike was the one who flinched. What kind of monster could do that to a child?

"It's okay," he repeated softly as he took a couple more slow steps toward the still-cowering boy. "No harm done."

When he reached out a hand toward Mickey, the boy recoiled even more. So Ike took a step in retreat. When he did, Mickey bolted away with the speed of a wild animal. One second he was there, the next he was gone. Ike supposed a kid learned to move quickly when he was living with devils.

A soft tread on the stairs brought Ike's attention back around. He wasn't surprised to see Annie descending, her bare feet padding softly on the sagging wooden planks.

"What happened?" she asked without preamble. Her voice was in no way accusatory or condemning. She simply wanted to know what had set Mickey off.

Ike pointed at the broken flashlight on the floor. "He pulled it out of the toolbox, and it was too heavy for him. I guess when it broke, he thought I was going to punish him for doing it."

She nodded as she descended the remaining two steps and retrieved a broom and dustpan from beneath the stairs. "Believe it or not, he's actually come a long way since he arrived at Homestead."

Ike took the broom from her and shooed her back to the steps. "Broken glass and bare feet," he said simply as he began to sweep up the mess. Then, without missing a beat, he asked, "You mean he used to be even more scared than that?"

Annie nodded. "Significantly. But now his nightmares don't come nearly as frequently as they used to, and he doesn't wet the bed as often as he did. And he used to always run away and hide for hours when something like this happened. Now he just goes to the living room window and stares out at the street."

"How long has he been here?"

"A little over a year now."

Which meant he'd been even smaller when he'd arrived, Ike thought. Had been smaller when his parents were whaling on him. Ike's stomach tightened into a knot.

"He's a good kid," he said as he swept the last of the glass into the dustpan.

"Yes, he is."

"He shouldn't have to have gone through what he did."

"No, he shouldn't have."

Ike really didn't think he wanted to know the answer to his next question, but he posed it anyway. "Do the rest of your kids come from similar backgrounds?"

She nodded again. "Most of them do, yes. Some actually have worse stories to tell."

Ike couldn't imagine much that was worse than being beaten within an inch of your life by your own parents.

Not until Annie told him, "A lot of them have been sexually abused, too. One of my kids was born with HIV. She didn't live to see her fourth birthday. I haven't taken on any really young kids since that."

Ike didn't want to hear any more. He didn't want to know that there were kids like that in the world. Didn't want to know that there were people who were capable of doing things like that to children. He wondered how Annie could stand it, being surrounded by that kind of thing everyday.

As if she knew exactly what he was thinking, she said quietly, "They're here with me because they don't have anyone else."

He looked over at her then, and for the first time since meeting her, he began to understand. It was just the way Annie was. Generous, loving, decent. He hadn't picked up on the qualities before because he simply hadn't recognized them. He didn't know any people who were that generous, loving and decent. At least, he hadn't. Not until now.

"What happens to your kids when they leave Homestead House?"

She smiled brightly. "Part of the program here is to enable them to do something productive with their lives once they leave Homestead—which they're required to do once they turn eighteen. A lot of them—more than half, as a matter of fact—have gone to college, frequently with scholarships. I have one girl who's at Penn State studying to be a veterinarian, and a boy who'll be graduating from Temple with a degree in Education this spring. Most of my other kids have found jobs in everything from retail to industrial. You know that new restaurant, The Rose Trellis?"

Ike nodded. "Yeah, I've tried a million times to get a reservation there, but they've never been able to accommodate me—the waiting list is a mile long. The place is supposed to have unbelievable food."

Annie grinned. "Malcolm, the chef there, is one of my kids."

"You're joking."

"Nope. That kid always was into everything in the kitchen. A fabulous cook. I really hated to see him go. Dinner hasn't been the same since."

Ike chuckled. "Do all your kids wind up having such happy endings?"

Her expression clouded. "No. Not always, unfortunately. One of my boys is currently doing time at Rahway for armed robbery and aggravated assault. And a few years ago, one of my girls took off one night. I haven't heard from her since. There have been a few other incidents, too, but usually my kids wind up in much better situations than they would have if they'd gone into state care.''

Ike didn't miss the fact that she still referred to the fallen of her brood with the possessive 'my.' He supposed Annie would always feel responsible for her children, regardless of the ways they chose to spend their lives. And she wouldn't turn her back on them just because they made the wrong choices. Such mistakes would only wound her and make her wonder where *she* went wrong.

"Would you like some lunch?'' she asked him suddenly, as if they'd been discussing nothing more consequential than the weather.

He emptied the dustpan into a nearby trash can. "Yeah, sure. Lunch sounds good.''

As he followed her back up the stairs, Ike tried not to notice the subtle sway of her hips or the way her faded jeans clung to her like a second skin. Tried, and failed miserably. So instead, he recalled the sad state of her basement, and that sobered him immediately.

"I know I've said it a million times already,'' he began, "and I know you hate to hear it, but, Annie, this place is in terrible shape.''

She looked over her shoulder and frowned at him, then opened her mouth to object.

Before she could do so, he interjected, "Beyond terrible. It's dangerous. You need to find a new place for your kids.''

"So what would you have me do?'' she demanded as they made their way toward the kitchen.

"Sell the place. Move out. Take your kids someplace where they won't have to play in the street. Where they'll have some fresh air to breathe for a change.''

She expelled a few humorless chuckles. "Oh, sure. No problem. I'd be lucky to get what I originally paid for this house if I put it up for sale, and the kind of place you describe would cost me ten times more.'' She spun around and settled her hands on her hips in challenge. "How many times do I have to tell you, Ike? I'd love to move my kids someplace else, but I *don't... have... the money.*"

"So how tough can it be to raise it?"

She shook her head in disbelief. "I've been running Homestead House for ten years now. In that length of time, I've spoken to every government official, every corporate big shot, every captain of industry, every charitable organization I can think of, stopping just short of dropping to my knees to beg for funding. In ten years of doing that, do you know how much money I've raised?"

He shook his head.

"Barely enough to keep *this* house up and running halfway effectively. If you knew how close I've come, how many times, to losing Homestead, to knowing these kids would wind up lost in the system or in foster homes with people who couldn't care less about them, or, worse, back with the families who were mistreating them to begin with..." She ran a hand through her hair and expelled an errant breath of air. "If you only knew."

She stopped, clearly reining in her anger by little more than a thread. She lowered her hand to her forehead, as if trying to ward off a migraine. "No one cares, Ike," she told him simply. "No one gives a damn that these kids need help. Everyone would just as soon pretend they don't exist. They'd rather not know that this kind of stuff happens. So they figure if they ignore it—if they ignore me—it'll all just go away."

Ike could hear the unspoken admonishment in her voice that he was precisely the kind of person she was describing. And guiltily, he recalled that not too long ago, he had been.

"But they're wrong," Annie continued relentlessly. "As long as ignorance and indifference like that exists, the abuse isn't going to go away." She paused for only a moment before adding, "And neither will I."

Her statement made, she turned toward the kitchen. "You want tuna fish or PB and J?"

Ike's head spun at her sudden change from vehement crusader to Betty Crocker. "Uh, tuna fish, I guess," he told her automatically.

"Fine."

The kitchen was crowded with children, ranging in age from what to Ike's untrained eye seemed very young to high school. Some sat around the table eating, some stood at the counter fixing lunch, some were obviously just hanging out, enjoying a leisurely Saturday afternoon. As he threaded his way through them to wash his hands at the kitchen sink, he noted that they laughed, chatted, and wolfed down sandwiches. They looked healthy, robust, clean and friendly. None seemed to be casualties of abuse or troubled in any way. They all seemed like normal, likable kids.

And that, Ike suspected, was because they had Annie.

Without her intervention, God only knew what kind of situations these kids would be in or where they would go from here. He assumed there had been scores of others just like them who had come and gone in the last ten years, since Homestead House had opened. How many lives had Annie and her late husband changed over the course of the years? How many had Annie changed since her husband's death? How many human beings were happy and productive in the world today instead of lost and troubled, simply because she had taken it upon herself to become involved?

Lots, he supposed. She'd influenced more lives than anyone he knew. Why did it bother him to realize that? he wondered. Then, immediately, he had an answer. Maybe it was because, in spite of her excelling at touching other people's lives, she seemed so unwilling to touch his.

Ike was thoughtful as he took a seat among the children to eat his sandwich. Absently, he answered their questions about himself and his work and his intentions for the house, and he discreetly fended off the flirtations of a girl who looked to be scarcely a teenager. All the while, he was acutely aware of Annie's eyes on him, and he couldn't help but feel that she was measuring him up. For what, he couldn't imagine. Could be she had some intentions for him. He smiled as he thought about that. He hoped Annie did have intentions for him. Because he sure as hell had some for her.

As he reached for the last of his potato chips, Ike smiled. Yeah, he had intentions, all right. He just hoped Annie was open to a little adventure.

Six

Annie stood in the middle of what passed for her back-yard—a tiny plot of half-dead grass measuring roughly ten feet by twelve—and shielded her eyes against the bright sunlight as she watched the man perched precariously near the gutter on her roof. There were actually four men up there, all of them methodically banging away like windup toys at the new shingles that sparkled under the noonday sun. But Annie was concerned for only one of them. Ike was going to get heatstroke if he didn't come down soon. Unlike the others, who'd shown up earlier that morning at a more respectable nine o'clock, he'd been up there working since dawn.

A full week had passed since he'd invaded her house with his announcement that he was going to set it to rights. Every single morning, rain or shine, Ike had arrived at her front door with the sun, armed with his ubiquitous tool-box, wearing his uniform of grubby jeans, T-shirt and work boots. Usually, he'd labored alone, on one solitary project at a time, like sealing the basement against water seepage, or reinforcing the stairs—all four flights of them—or painting the bedrooms—all eight of them.

Then, gradually, something rather miraculous had happened. When Ike had asked Annie's older kids, free from school for the summer, to lend a hand, they had easily and without argument fallen into step beside him. They'd painted the hallways, the stairwells, the bathrooms and the public rooms. The bigger boys had waxed the floors. The girls had washed the windows. Somehow, no one had been immune to Ike's enthusiasm.

Even Mickey had made himself useful by appointing himself Ike's assistant, whether Ike wanted one or not. The little boy had carted around the toolbox that was far too heavy for him, and had made Ike illustrate the use of each and every tool inside. Then he'd behaved like a surgical assistant, doling out whatever instrument Ike needed when the bigger man called it out.

After that, Ike had started talking about bigger projects, using words like *rewiring* and *drywall* and *roof*. Annie had told him to forget about it, that projects like those cost lots and lots of money that she didn't have. But Ike had assured her he had lots and lots of friends in the construction business who'd be more than happy to contribute their time if not the actual materials, which, he had added with a smile, he could get for her wholesale.

Annie was pretty certain the only reason Ike's friends had acquiesced to donating their time and materials had been because Ike had bullied or bribed them, or called in favors too numerous to count. But she wasn't about to stop him. Regardless of the reason for his newfound humanitarianism, there was no way she was going to say no to all the work he had offered. It was something to benefit her kids, after all.

All in all, she thought now as she anxiously nibbled a hangnail on her thumb and willed him not to fall to his death, Ike had gone above and beyond the call of duty, a duty she'd never called upon him to perform in the first place. It was odd behavior, to say the least, for a man who had as much admitted that he thought what Annie did for a living was a waste of time. Odder still for a man who professed to dislike children. And especially odd for a man who wished he could overlook and forget about the kids, like hers, who came from disadvantaged backgrounds.

So what gave? she wondered. Why had the man taken vacation time he could have idled away on a powdery white beach fringed with gracefully arching palm trees, and used it instead to grunt and sweat in physical labor in the middle of the concrete jungle?

Not that she minded his grunting and sweating, she thought before she could stop herself. Her gaze wandered involuntarily over his profile, noting the way his white-blond hair, looking almost silver at the moment so saturated with perspiration was it, dangled over his forehead as he concentrated on his work. Somewhere along the line, he had stripped off his T-shirt, and his back and torso were slick with moisture, muscles dancing every time the hammer fell. His shoulders were pink, in danger of burning, but she couldn't quite bring herself to warn him. Because she knew he'd put his shirt on again if she did.

Annie swallowed hard and forced herself to look away. There was no way she could deny that he had been a godsend, the way he had slaved for the last seven days. But she had to face facts. And the fact was that Ike Guthrie was *no* a man who volunteered freely to help out his fellow human being. So why did he keep coming around to help out Annie and her kids?

"You guys want to break for some lemonade?" she called up to the men.

Immediately, three hammers ceased, three men wiped their wringing-wet brows and three men nodded in the absolute affirmative. Only Ike continued to pound away, as if he hadn't even heard her question.

"Hey, Ike!" Annie called out more loudly.

Finally, he, too, quit hammering, glancing down at her quickly, as if he'd forgotten where he was. "What?" he called back.

"Take a breather, will ya? I've made some lemonade and sandwiches. Come on down before you dehydrate." He started to shake his head, so Annie quickly added, "Now. Come down now."

It was the tone of voice she normally reserved for her kids when they were behaving like undisciplined animals, but it seemed to work equally well on overzealous adults. Ike nodded, picked up his shirt and wiped his dripping face with it, then tossed it aside again and headed for the ladder. The old wooden monstrosity seemed in no way steady when he climbed onto it, so Annie crossed the yard to hold the ladder still while Ike made his way down.

The view, she noted as she watched his descent, was quite extraordinary. His ragged jeans were filthy and streaked with tar, but they molded to his thighs and buttocks like nobody's business. She fancied she could see the bunching and relaxing of every solid muscle in the man's lower half as he drew nearer, and sweat trickled down his back—also filthy and streaked with tar—in slow, meticulous rivulets. Out of nowhere, Annie wondered what he would taste like right then if she kissed him. Immediately, she closed her eyes and willed the thought away.

She opened them again when she felt Ike come to a solid landing on the ground beside her. He seemed like such a giant compared to her, easily a foot taller than she. Even with her head tipped back, she found herself staring at his neck, and she wondered when that part of a man had become such a sexual turn-on to her. The musky scent of him surrounded her, and she found herself wanting to bury her lips in the damp hollow at the base of his throat.

She had to get over this crazy preoccupation with Ike Guthrie, she told herself. Her dreams alone this week had been erotic enough to make her certifiable. He was just some guy who was helping her out, she reminded herself. Some guy who was totally confusing and arousing as hell, granted, but still just some guy. She'd be better off remembering that, and not wondering what he wore under his blue jeans . . . if anything at all.

"Annie, unless you're planning to kiss me, it's probabl[y] not a good idea for you to look at me like that."

Her attention snapped back at his roughly uttered warn[n]ing. "Like what?" she asked softly.

"Like you're wondering what I'd taste like with a littl[e] cocktail sauce on the side."

She felt her face become hot, and tried to convince her self it was a result of the sun. Unfortunately, she knew bet ter.

"I wasn't thinking that," she denied quietly.

"Weren't you?"

She shook her head and pressed her lips shut to kee[p] from revealing that she'd had garlic butter more in min[d] than cocktail sauce. "Uh-uh," she finally trusted herself t[o] say.

Ike nodded, but somehow she knew it wasn't because h[e] was accepting her assurance. "I see," he murmured.

He lifted his hand to her hair and twined a long length o[f] it around his finger. Then he dipped his head down until hi[s] lips were a scant inch from her own. Instinctively, Anni[e] tilted her own head back in preparation for a kiss.

"I believe you mentioned...lemonade," he sai[d] smoothly as he straightened, turning loose of her hair. H[e] smiled mischievously. "And lunch. Sounds good. I'm.. starving."

Oh, like she was really going to fall for that old line, An nie thought. That stupid hunger double entendre. He'd al ready tried that on her once, and it hadn't worked. Well not really. Not much. Men were just so certain they coul[d] get whatever they wanted from women if they referred t[o] it in terms of food. She, however, was too smart for tha[t] this time.

Then, when she realized she still stood poised to receiv[e] a kiss Ike hadn't even offered her to begin with, sh[e] frowned. With as much nonchalance as she could muste[r] she relaxed a little, shifting her weight from one foot to th[e] other.

"Um," she began eloquently. But for some reason, she found it impossible to finish the sentiment.

"Um," Ike echoed with a grin.

She arched a brow and turned silently away, following the route the other men had already taken into the house. Ike trailed closely behind her the whole way, and as she always could when he stood or walked behind her, Annie felt his eyes taking inventory of every body part she owned. He might as well have been touching every body part, too, she thought, so thorough was his inspection, and so fiercely did he rattle her. She glanced down at her baggy, thrift store madras shorts and equally bedraggled T-shirt. Once again, her clothing was in no way revealing. So why did she suddenly feel as if she were walking around naked?

"You know, you've been feeding me a lot this week," Ike said as he followed her through the back door. "Why don't you let me return the favor tonight?"

Annie spun around to face him. "You're kidding, right?"

He seemed genuinely surprised. "Of course I'm not kidding. I owe you. Let me take you to dinner."

"*You* owe *me*? Don't you think you have that backward?" Without even giving him a chance to answer the question, she added, "I don't even recognize my house, because you've made it such a nice place. The basement doesn't leak anymore, the toilet doesn't sound like it's going to explode every time you flush it, those weird brown stains on the living room ceiling that always made me jump because I thought they were spiders are gone . . ."

"But, Annie—"

"The floors used to squeak so loudly at night, it sounded like every ghost in the tri-state area was learning to ballroom dance on them, but you fixed that, too."

"Yes, but, Annie—"

"You also fixed the radiators in the dining room, you fixed the front porch, you fixed that ceiling fan in the family room that's *never* worked before. You even fixed my old computer that's so obsolete they don't make parts for it anymore.''

"But, Annie—''

"You don't owe *me* anything, Ike. *I'm* the one who's never going to be able to repay you."

He smiled rakishly, and she decided at once it wasn't a good thing. "Sure you can," he said smoothly.

She eyed him narrowly. "How?''

"Have dinner with me tonight."

"But you don't owe me anything," she repeated half-heartedly, wondering why she fought so ferociously to deny this man, when deep down she wanted to give him everything. "You don't. You've fixed everything here."

His smile fell some as he shook his head. "I haven't fixed everything, Annie."

"Yes, you have. You've—''

"Not everything," he repeated. "But I'm working on it."

His statement confused her, but she didn't take time to consider it. She was too caught up in the way he was looking at her, too befuddled by the way his eyes seemed to see right into her soul. What could possibly be left in Homestead House that needed fixing? she wondered. He'd taken care of everything.

"Just give me a little more time," he added softly. "And have dinner with me tonight."

"I don't think I can . . .''

He took a slow step forward and lifted a hand to her cheek, skimming it open-palm down to the side of her neck where her pulse jumped erratically. "I know this great place. Quiet, intimate, an incredible view. Unbelievably good food, and a tremendous wine selection. You'll like it. I promise."

His hand cupped her nape, and a hot shiver wound through her entire body. "Well, I don't know . . .''

"I'm very well acquainted with the owner," he added. "He'll make sure we get whatever we want. We'll have our pick of tables. Something nice and secluded."

"Gee, I . . ." She swallowed hard, unable to quite get the words out to tell him no.

"Come on, Annie." Ike stroked his thumb leisurely over her pulse. "Let yourself out once in a while. You've been working too hard lately. Nobody's going to mind if you have fun this once."

Annie knew it wasn't a good idea. She knew it would be a big mistake to go anywhere quiet and intimate or nice and secluded with Ike. The last time she'd been with him in a similar scenario, things had gotten out of hand. She'd forgotten who she was for a moment. And as a result, she'd nearly made a terrible mistake. She opened her mouth to give him an unequivocal no.

And heard herself say, "Okay."

Ike jumped on her agreement before she could rescind it by telling her, "I'll pick you up at eight."

"Isn't that too late . . . for dinner, I mean?"

He smiled cryptically. "No, Annie. It's never too late."

Before she could ask him to clarify that for her, he turned and joined his co-workers in the kitchen. Annie was left alone in the hall to wonder what she'd just gotten herself into, how she was going to get herself out of it again—and what she should wear to dinner in an intimate, secluded place.

The elevator doors unfolded on what Ike considered to be one of the poshest, most comfortable, most tastefully furnished rooms he'd ever had the pleasure to visit. The ivory marble floor was complemented nicely by three walls of honey-colored, burled walnut paneling, and one wall of floor-to-ceiling windows that looked out onto the Philadelphia skyline. A pair of standing brass lamps with creamy glass shades provided the only illumination for the room, bathing it in a hazy golden glow that seemed to soften everything. The furnishings were an eclectic mix of leather and fabric, the former buff in color, the latter an intriguing matrimony of geometric design and bold stripe in golds and browns.

It was rich, voluptuous and masculine. It was a place Ike called home.

Before he could escort her from the elevator, Annie spun around and narrowed her eyes at him in accusation. "When you said we were going up to the penthouse, I thought you meant we'd be in some revolving restaurant with a breathtaking view of the city."

Ike shrugged and pretended not to understand. "That is a breathtaking view of the city. Just because the room doesn't revolve doesn't mean—"

Annie frowned as she interrupted him. "This is your apartment, isn't it?"

"My condo," he corrected her with a smile, opening his hand at the small of her back to gently prod her out of the elevator. He extracted the tiny key from the button board, exited behind Annie, then closed the elevator again by inserting the key into another opening beside the doors inside his apartment. As the brass doors folded closed behind them, he pocketed the key in the trousers of his charcoal suit. "Welcome to Chez Ike," he said, sweeping his hand into the silent room, empty save their own presence. "Best food in town."

"I should have known you'd pull something like this."

He feigned confusion again. "Something like what?"

Annie crossed her arms over her black cocktail dress— the one she'd been wearing the night he'd been purchased for her, Ike recalled fondly—and tapped her foot menacingly.

"Something like taking me hostage," she accused him through gritted teeth.

"Hostage? Why, Annie, you can't be serious. I would never do something like that."

"I notice I can't call the elevator back unless I have that key you just dropped into your pants pocket."

He spread his arms open wide and smiled devilishly. "You're welcome to come and get it any time you want to."

She made a face at him. "Thanks, but I'll wait until you've had too much to drink and pass out in your pasta."

"I never drink to excess. The only place I plan on passing out tonight is in your arms, and only because you've exhausted me with your demands for more."

"Ike—"

"For more dessert," he clarified.

She frowned harder.

"It's cheesecake," he cajoled her. "Remember how good it was the last time we had it? In Cape May?" he added when her glare only intensified.

"If memory serves," she muttered, "I left mine untouched."

"Oh, it wasn't quite untouched," he reminded her. "You had a few bites, remember? Enough to let you know you were missing something extraordinary by leaving it there on the plate that way. The serving I had was unbelievably tasty." He cupped his hand beneath Annie's elbow, much as he had done a month ago in Cape May when he'd escorted her to dinner. "But I didn't get to finish that night, either. So tonight, just to be sure that doesn't happen again, let's have dessert first."

Annie allowed herself to be led into Ike's domain, but assured him to the contrary, "I don't think so."

"Don't want to spoil your girlish figure, is that it?"

For the first time since they'd arrived, Annie smiled. It wasn't quite a happy smile, Ike noted, but at least she seemed to be getting into the spirit of things a bit.

"That's it exactly," she said before turning her back on him and finding her own way to the sofa. "Boy, something smells wonderful," she added, lifting her nose to enjoy the aroma. "I thought you said you hate to cook."

Ike had left a bottle of Chenin Blanc chilling on the glass coffee table before he'd left, and now the silver ice bucket was cold and sweaty, dripping with condensation that glowed like liquid topaz in the faint light. With all the finesse and confidence of a five-star wine captain, he extracted the bottle and opened it, then splashed a generous amount into two delicate-looking crystal stems. Silently, he handed one to Annie. She accepted it, but didn't sample the wine.

"I told you the food here was great," he responded to her earlier observation.

"When did you have time to prepare something?"

"I didn't. If I was doing the cooking, no one would ever eat here. Including me."

He lifted his glass to make a toast, but before he could do so, a door to their right opened, and a man entered the living room. He was tall, lanky and young-looking, and his black hair was caught in a long ponytail at his nape. His peacock blue jacket was the only spot of color on an otherwise black ensemble—black baggy trousers, black collarless shirt, black, pointy-toed shoes. A sapphire stickpin nearly as blue as his eyes winked at his throat, while another, smaller sapphire was fastened in his earlobe.

"Everything's set to go, Ike," he said as he approached the couple. "Just turn everything off in ten minutes, and dinner is served. Is this Annie?"

Ike nodded. "This is Annie."

The man smiled and extended his hand. "Hi. I'm Ike's cousin, Raymond."

"Raymond's studying to be a chef," Ike told her. "And he's been experimenting on the family lately. Tonight, it's my turn."

"My pork medallions are to die for," he said with a smile. "But Ike insisted on lighter fare. I hope you like shrimp."

Annie, clearly surprised by the newcomer, took his hand in hers and smiled. "Uh, hi," she said. "And I love shrimp."

"Then you're in for a treat," Raymond told her with unabashed pride. He turned to pat Ike on the shoulder. "Light on the garlic," he added with a smile, "just like you asked."

"Thanks, Ray," Ike told him.

"No sweat. Nice to meet you, Annie," Raymond added as he made his way to the brass doors on the other side of the room. He extracted a key ring from his pocket, inserted a small key to summon the elevator, then stepped on and waved goodbye as the doors folded closed over him.

"He has his own key to the place?" Annie asked.

Ike nodded. "He cooks for me a lot. He's going to be extremely successful someday. And just like your Malcolm, you'll be able to say you knew Raymond when."

"So when do we eat?" she asked.

"That hungry, are you?"

"Ike . . ."

He smiled. She was rattled. Good. So was he. "First, I want to make a toast." He extended his glass toward her, half expecting her to ignore the motion.

Although she did indeed seem reluctant to hear what he wanted to salute, she slowly lifted her glass to within inches of his.

"To us," he said softly, touching the lip of his glass to hers with a soft *ping*. "To getting acquainted."

Annie's eyes were the color of the ocean in this light, Ike thought vaguely, and very nearly as deep. "I thought we were already acquainted," she said softly.

He shook his head. "Not nearly enough. Not as well as we're going to be."

With his toast—and intentions—made clear, Ike tipped his glass toward hers one final time before lifting it to his lips and filling his mouth with the wine.

Annie, he noted, was much slower to complete the gesture. But after a moment of watching him closely, and apparent consideration for what he had said, she, too, raised her glass, though not quite as high as Ike had.

"To us," she echoed in a quiet voice. She sipped slowly, her eyelids fluttering closed as she savored the wine more completely. When she opened them again, her pupils were larger, her eyes seeming darker as a result. "To getting acquainted," she added. Finally, almost as an afterthought, she whispered again, "To us."

Seven

Annie stared at the generous slice of cheesecake Ike had placed before her and wondered again what she was doing here alone with him in his apartment. *Condo,* she reminded herself quickly. This wasn't an apartment he rented. He owned this incredible place.

She didn't think she'd ever seen a home more beautiful than Ike's. Even her sister Sophie, whose funds were limitless and whose taste was excellent, hadn't managed to capture in her suburban mansion the aura of wealth and refinement that surrounded Ike so naturally. It struck Annie again how very different the two of them were, and how utterly opposite Ike was from the man she had loved and married. She could never feel at home in a place like this. Nor could she imagine a child being able to thrive in such surroundings. There were too many things that screamed, "Hands off!" Too many things in the living room alone that were clearly not intended for, well, living.

Then again, she thought, that wasn't surprising. Ike was a bachelor who probably didn't even spend that much time

PLAY

SILHOUETTE'S

LUCKY HEARTS

GAME

AND YOU GET

- ★ **FREE BOOKS**
- ★ **A FREE GIFT**
- ★ **AND MUCH MORE**

TURN THE PAGE AND DEAL YOURSELF IN →

PLAY "LUCKY HEARTS" AND GET ...

★ **Exciting Silhouette Desire® novels—FREE**

★ **PLUS a lovely Austrian Crystal Necklace—FREE**

THEN CONTINUE YOUR LUCKY STREAK WITH A SWEETHEART OF A DEAL

1. Play Lucky Hearts as instructed on the opposite page.

2. Send back this card and you'll receive brand-new Silhouette Desire® novels. These books have a cover price of $3.50 each, but they are yours to keep absolutely free.

3. There's no catch. You're under no obligation to buy anything. We charge nothing — ZERO — for your first shipment. And you don't have to make any minimum number of purchases — not even one!

4. The fact is thousands of readers enjoy receiving books by mail from the Silhouette Reader Service. They like the convenience of home delivery...they like getting the best new novels month before they're available in stores...and they love our discount prices!

5. We hope that after receiving your free books you'll want to remain a subscriber. But the choice is yours — to continue or cancel, anytime at all! So why not take us up on our invitation, with no risk of any kind. You'll be glad you did!

You'll look like a million dollars when you wear this lovely necklace! Its cobra-link chain is a generous 18" long, and the multi-faceted Austrian crystal sparkles like a diamond!

NOT ACTUAL SIZE

SILHOUETTE'S

With a coin— scratch off the silver card and check below to see what we have for you.

YES! I have scratched off the silver card. Please send me all the free books and gift for which I qualify. I understand that I am under no obligation to purchase any books, as explained on the back and on the opposite page.

225 CIS AZH5 (U-SIL-D-06/96)

NAME _____

ADDRESS _____ APT. _____

CITY _____ STATE _____ ZIP _____

Twenty-one gets you 4 free books, and a free Austrian crystal necklace

Twenty gets you 4 free books

Nineteen gets you 3 free books

Eighteen gets you 2 free books

Offer limited to one per household and not valid to current Silhouette Desire® subscribers. All orders subject to approval.

© 1990 HARLEQUIN ENTERPRISES LIMITED.   **PRINTED IN U.S.A.**

BUSINESS REPLY MAIL
FIRST-CLASS MAIL   PERMIT NO. 717   BUFFALO, NY

POSTAGE WILL BE PAID BY ADDRESSEE

SILHOUETTE READER SERVICE
3010 WALDEN AVE
PO BOX 1867
BUFFALO NY 14240-9952

NO POSTAGE
NECESSARY
IF MAILED
IN THE
UNITED STATES

at home. Certainly he hadn't had a family of any kind in mind when he'd furnished this place. Nor did it seem likely that he intended to introduce a wife and kids into the picture in the future.

So what did Annie think she was doing, sitting there sharing a table with him, and wondering what it would be like to spend the night?

She sighed and pushed her dessert away without even sampling it, then rested her elbows on the table and cupped her chin in one hand.

"Why did you invite me over here tonight?" she asked bluntly.

Ike waited until he had finished pouring them both a cup of coffee to reply. "I thought the reason was obvious."

Annie shook her head. "Nope. Sorry. I've been over it a million times in my head since you showed up at my door last weekend, and I can't for the life of me figure out why you've barged into my life, why you've gone out of your way to fix up my house, and why you're wining and dining me with such utter care. It doesn't make any sense."

He cocked an eyebrow in question. "Doesn't it?"

"Nope," she repeated. "It doesn't."

"I've been hanging around your house all week, because you need help and I'm able to offer it," he told her. "But the reason I invited you to dinner tonight is much more personal, and much more selfish." He paused to lift his coffee cup to his lips for an idle sip, then replaced it in the saucer. He, too, settled an elbow on the table, resting his chin in his hand in exactly the same way Annie had. "I invited you to dinner tonight, Annie, because I want to make love to you."

For some reason, his point-blank reply didn't startle her. Maybe, not so deep down, she had known from the start what he would be wanting, even expecting, once he had her alone on his own turf. And maybe, not so deep down, she had come along for the ride for precisely the same reason. Ever since that night in Cape May, Annie had been turning over in her mind Ike's suggestion that she shied away from him because she felt as if she were betraying her husband. At first, she'd thought the idea was ludicrous. But after a while, she had begun to wonder if maybe Ike wasn't right.

Mark had been dead for five years. And in that time, more than one man had made it clear to Annie that he wanted to get to know her better. She'd always told herself she wasn't interested because none of the men was interesting. Then she'd met Ike. A man who was good-looking, articulate and intelligent. A man who had built up a very successful business and lived a very luxurious life. A man who could make her laugh and make her think. A very interesting man, indeed. Yet she'd pushed him away, too.

And all because, for one small moment, he'd touched off a spark of life inside her that she'd been certain had died along with her husband. Why was it so terrible for her to feel alive again? she wondered. What was so bad about feeling so good?

"Annie?"

Ike's voice came to her as if from very far away. She remembered then that she hadn't yet responded to his plainly spoken desire.

"I see," she said softly, reaching for her coffee cup.

"That's all you have to say?" he asked. " 'I see?' "

She lifted a shoulder in a halfhearted shrug. "What else would you have me say?"

"Oh, gee, I don't know. How about something along the lines of, 'Okay, Ike. Where's the bedroom? I just so happen to have worn something under this dress that you're going to find very intriguing.' "

Annie's smile was more than a little nervous. "How about we take things a bit more slowly?" she suggested. "Maybe start in the living room, enjoying the view or something."

Ike's smile was more than a little suggestive. "Or something."

She scooted her chair away from the table and rose before he could come around and assist her. She didn't want him any closer than necessary for the moment, because she was still disconcerted by the questions she'd left unanswered in her brain. Having Ike so near only confounded her more, so she moved quickly to the bank of windows on the other side of the room.

"Oh, you have a telescope," she said when she noted the instrument tucked into a corner.

Ike nodded. "You'd be amazed how educational they can be."

She bent to peer through it, and was surprised to find it was tipped up toward an apartment in the high rise across the street. When she looked at Ike again, she hoped her expression was properly chastising. "Don't tell me you've been acting like Jimmy Stewart in *Rear Window*. You don't actually look into other people's apartments with this thing. Do you?"

"I promise you, Annie, I only use that thing to observe heavenly bodies."

She shook her head ruefully. "Shame on you. I'm glad I live on the other side of town."

"I'm not."

"Let's not get into that again," she said. She refused to spoil their evening by going over something they were never going to settle.

"I just meant—"

"Forget it, Ike. Let's talk about something else."

"All right. Let's talk about you."

"What about me?"

He smiled. "You didn't eat your dessert."

"My girlish figure, remember?"

"How could I forget? I've been completely preoccupied with thoughts of it since I first saw you in that little black dress."

She'd never considered the long-sleeved, scooped-neck dress to be particularly revealing. The hem fell just below her knees, the neckline well above her breasts. It did fit a little snugly, but was by no means tight. It was, to Annie's way of thinking, an elegant, but very unremarkable, dress.

Nevertheless, she heard herself ask, "What do you mean?"

Only when Ike began to close the small distance between them did she realize how thoroughly she'd backed herself into a corner—literally. To her left was a plate glass window that rose thirty-four stories above the city. Behind her was a paneled wall, polished to a high gloss, but completely unrelenting. And to her right was a thick-trunked palm tree potted in a heavy brass planter, the combination rising to a height even taller than her own.

"I mean," he told her softly as he approached her, "that your dress reveals more than it conceals."

"But it covers up—"

"Nothing," he interrupted. "And enhances everything."

Ike strode forward slowly, smiling when Annie took a step in retreat to match each of his in pursuit. His approach continued unhindered until he had backed her against the wall. And before she could escape, he quickly planted a forearm against the wall on each side of her head. Annie flattened herself along the wall as much as she could, so Ike flattened himself along her, insinuating a muscular thigh between both of hers.

He felt her all along the length of him, could feel her small breasts rising and falling against his chest as she gasped for breath, could feel her flat belly pressing into his arousal. If either one of them moved, even the tiniest bit, he thought, he couldn't be held responsible for what happened as a result.

He dipped his head until he could press his forehead to hers. "There hasn't been anyone since your husband, has there, Annie? It's been five years since you've been with a man, hasn't it?"

She swallowed hard and inhaled deeply, the action only bringing her body into closer contact with his. Her eyelids fluttered closed, as if she, too, felt the unholy heat that spiraled throughout his body.

"Um, that depends on what you mean by 'been with,' "
she whispered. "Actually, if you take it in literal terms, I've
been with lots of men. Every day. I've been with them in
delis when I have to grab lunch on the run, in supermar-
kets when I'm buying groceries, in shopping malls
when—"

"In bed," Ike interrupted her. "Have you been with a
man in bed?" When she didn't reply, he took great pleasure in clarifying. "Have you been with a man in bed, naked, hot and aroused, with him buried so deep inside you
that you didn't know where you ended and he began, telling him to go deeper, harder, faster, longer—"

He halted abruptly at the strangled little sound she uttered. Then he moved against her, rubbed the long length
of himself as intimately into her softness as he dared. The
thigh he had thrust between her legs rose higher, then lowered, then rose again. Annie's pelvis shifted in response, her
movement mimicking his, as if she weren't...quite...
satisfied with his ministrations.

"Five years," he repeated when he trusted his voice not
to falter. "You haven't been with a man that way in five
years, have you, Annie?"

She swallowed hard again. "No." The one-word response was scarcely a whisper this time.

"Then I think it's about time you were."

"Ike..."

"Shh," he murmured as he turned his head to the side.

He slanted his mouth over hers and kissed her, running
the tip of his tongue along the length of her lower lip before slipping it inside her mouth. Immediately, she locked
hers with his, stroking against him as if she were intent on
devouring him alive.

Ike dropped his hand to her hip, pressing his fingers into
her thigh, urging them lower until he found the hem of her
skirt. Immediately, he bunched the fabric in his hand, then
dragged it and his fingers back up along her heated flesh,
lifting her leg to curl it around him. He skimmed his fingertips back along her leg until he encountered the cotton

of her panties. Not to be put off by so fragile a barrier, he pulled the fabric away and let his hand wander on a more intimate exploration.

"Oh, Ike," Annie moaned. "You shouldn't..."

"But I think I will anyway," he murmured back. He buried his face in the warm, fragrant skin of her neck and shoulder, nipping her lightly with his teeth, laving the wound with his tongue when she softly cried out.

She tore his necktie free from his collar, then reached for the buttons of his shirt, hastily unfastening them one by one until she could spread the garment open wide. As she tangled her fingers in the soft blond hair on his chest, Ike shrugged out of his shirt and jacket completely, then went to work on her dress. He fumbled with the back zipper twice, cursing his fingers for failing him now. As he'd suspected, she wore no brassiere underneath, so when he slowly pushed the dress over her shoulders and down her arms, Annie stood before him in the moonlight, half naked and fully aroused.

Boy, had he been remiss in thinking her too small and insignificant, Ike thought now. Her breasts were exquisite, round and firm with pale pink peaks, and perfectly sized for his palms. He reached for one, covering it with his hand, then closed his fingers gently around her soft flesh. Her eyes fluttered closed, her cheeks turning rosy in the scarce light.

"Why are you doing this to me?" she asked him.

Ike shook his head. Deep down in his heart, in his soul, he was pretty sure he knew the answer to that question. But he wasn't ready to voice it out loud. Saying it would make it too real too soon. He still didn't understand his actions completely. How could he possibly explain them to Annie?

"Because you've been driving me crazy since I laid eyes on you," he said truthfully. "Because I can't sleep at night, I can't eat, I can't concentrate on anything.... You've got me tied in knots. I can't seem to get you out of my system.

I can no more keep this from happening than I can stop the morning from coming."

"And the morning will come, too," Annie said softly. "Soon. What happens after that, Ike?"

He shook his head again. He couldn't think about that right now. All he could think about was making love to Annie. If she denied him this, he supposed he could live with her decision. Probably not long, but he could live with it. He only hoped her denial wouldn't come. He only hoped that he was right in his conviction that she wanted this as badly as he did.

When he didn't respond to her question, she nodded, seemingly as if she were no closer to knowing the answer than he was. For one long moment, the two of them only stood silent in the semidarkness, each waiting to see what the other would do. Annie was the first to move. She lifted a hand to Ike's belt and slowly, methodically, freed the length of leather from its buckle.

"Annie," he whispered as she unfastened the button of his trousers. The word was lost when he pressed his mouth to hers once again.

Slowly, as if taking great care, she lowered his zipper, then deftly slipped her hand inside. She found him at once, rock hard and ready for her, then jerked her hand away, as if fearful of her discovery. Immediately, Ike circled her wrist with strong fingers, urging her hand back to its exploration. With tentative, featherlike touches, Annie moved her fingers against him. Ike grew still at her caresses, then shuddered as she gradually grew bolder. Finally, she cupped as much of him in her palm as she could and rubbed the long length of him lustily.

"That's it," he ground out hoarsely, grabbing her wrist again. "That's enough."

"But I was just getting started," she purred, trying to free her hand from his grasp to retrieve her trophy again.

"Nope, sorry. Gotta take a break for a minute. Trust me."

To halt her objection, he took her mouth with his again, teasing the corners with his tongue, tracing the outline of her lips with its tip. Annie groaned and went limp, and Ike took advantage of her lazy posture to sweep her into his arms.

"What are you doing?" she asked dreamily as she settled her head against his shoulder.

"I'm taking you to bed."

It wasn't a good idea. The rational half of Annie's brain knew that, even if the emotional half didn't. Unfortunately, she'd never much heeded her sense of reason. She was and always had been ruled by her heart. She told herself that was why she was such a good social worker. It was also, she knew, what had gotten her into this mess with Ike to begin with.

But was it really a mess, she wondered? How long had it been since she'd felt this strongly, this intensely, about anything other than her kids? How long had it been since she'd allowed herself to enjoy something for herself this much? Annie had spent the last five years of her life doing for other people and denying herself. Why shouldn't she have a little excitement, a little pleasure, for a change? What was wrong with that?

For a moment, she thought she remembered something that was indeed wrong with that. For a moment, at the very edge of her consciousness, she almost realized a reason why she should tell Ike she couldn't make love with him. Then he curved his hand over her derriere as he lowered her onto his bed and insinuated his fingers between her thighs.

And after that, Annie couldn't think at all. She could only feel. A hot, heavy, urgent desire flickered to life in her midsection and quickly spiraled outward like paper in fire. Every nerve in her body seemed to burst into flame as Ike closed his lips over her breast and began to hungrily suckle her. Somewhere along the line, he'd shed the remainder of their clothing, and now he came to her as naked as she. Annie tangled her fingers in his silky hair and held his head against her bosom, murmuring alternately to halt his eager onslaught and never to let it end.

She opened her eyes long enough to appreciate how the moonlight tumbling through the window near the bed shadowed, then silvered, every muscle on his back. Her gaze dipped lower, to his taut buttocks and the backs of his hard thighs, then she closed her eyes again with a groan. She couldn't remember the last time she'd seen a man naked. And certainly never a man like him.

When she loosened her grip on his hair, she felt Ike's lips move lower, to the underside of her breasts and her concave belly. She giggled breathlessly when he dipped his tongue into her navel for a taste, but her laughter ceased when he tucked a hand between her thighs and parted her legs for a more intimate exploration. She opened her mouth to tell him to stop, not to go any further than he already had. But the words caught in her throat when she felt the tip of his tongue flicker against her as softly as a butterfly's dance.

She'd never felt such exquisite pleasure before. For long moments, Annie could only lay motionless, her fingers tangled in the sheets, her head turned into the pillow. But when the pressure of Ike's mouth grew more insistent, his exploration more thorough, she couldn't remain still. Gradually, ripples of delight began to unravel her, swelling little by little into velvet-crested waves of ecstasy. An explosion of sensation rocked her, and she cried out in wonder at the intoxicating newness of her feelings.

"Oh," she murmured as she felt his lips travel up the length of her torso again. "Oh, Ike . . ."

"So much for the appetizer," he whispered, his own voice sounding weak and more than a little strained. "Now we move on to the main course."

"I . . . I thought we were supposed to be having dessert," she managed to whisper.

"Oh, we will," he assured her softly. "We will. But first there's something I need to, uh, see to."

In her dazed state, Annie could think of little other than the fulfillment she craved so desperately. "Mmm," she murmured. "What's that?"

Her eyes had fluttered closed, and she found she didn't have the strength to open them. But she felt Ike reach to the side of the bed, heard the scrape of a drawer and the unmistakable whisper of plastic.

"Oh, that," she said, thankful that one of them, anyway, had had the foresight to remember. "Sex in the nineties," she added wistfully, thinking she should be more worried about endangering her heart than her body.

"Sex in the nineties," he agreed. "But that doesn't mean it has to be any less... enjoyable."

Annie was about to agree with him, but lost her voice when he buried his head between her breasts and launched a rather... eager... assault on her senses. After that, she pretty much lost herself in sensation. Ike seemed to surround her and invade her, filling every empty place inside her that had been cold and lifeless for so long. He tangled his fingers in her hair and rose above her, settling himself between her legs where she still ached with wanting him. She felt the heat and dampness of him all along her body, scarcely able to tell where, or even if, they became separate beings again.

And then he was inside her, deeper and more completely than she had ever imagined a man could be. He reached and warmed parts of her she hadn't even known could feel. Then he withdrew and dived more deeply still. Annie gasped at the fierceness of his possession, clasped her arms more tightly around him, hugged him to her with a passion she'd never felt before, and let him sweep her away.

The slow burn that had ignited within her quickly burst into a white explosion of heat. Just when she thought she could no longer tolerate his invasion, Ike turned so that he was on his back with Annie sitting astride him. He gripped her hips with firm hands and bucked under her, bringing another cry of delight from somewhere deep within her

hen he, too, cried out, stilling in an eager arch beneath
er, gasping as his essence erupted with hers.

Their descent was slow, reluctant and incomplete. An-
ie still felt as if she teetered on the edge of fulfillment, and
vondered if a single night would be enough to make up for
ive long years of wanting. She moved until she lay quiet
nd motionless beside Ike, facing him, trailing her index
inger along the length of his slick torso. His chest rose and
ell in an irregular rhythm, and he caught her hand in his,
olding it over his heart. His pulse leapt and raced like a
ral animal.

"Feel that?" he asked her. "That's what you've done to
e. My heart will never be the same again."

She smiled as she flattened her palm over the center of his
est. "Good. It's only fair. I shouldn't be the only one."

He rolled onto his side and opened his hand over her
art, grinning back at her when he realized her heartbeat
as every bit as uneven as his own. For a moment, they
nly lay side by side, hands over each other's hearts, lost in
discovery neither was quite sure how to deal with.

Then Ike broke the silence by asking, "What time do you
ave to be home?"

"By two," she replied immediately, already pretty cer-
in she knew what his next question would be.

"Want to do it again?"

Annie laughed, a low, sultry sound she could scarcely
lieve had emerged from her. "Yes," she replied just as
iickly. "And again, and again, and again, and—"

Ike silenced her with a kiss. "We'll need more than one
ght for that."

"Okay."

"Lots and lots of nights."

"Okay."

"Starting tomorrow."

"Okay."

"Annie?"

"Yes?"

"Are you always this agreeable?"

"Only when I'm getting what I want."

Ike smiled. "Then I guess I'll have to make sure you always get what you want."

"I guess you will."

"Fortunately for both of us, I know *exactly* what you want."

She curled her arm around his neck and pulled him toward her again. "Then why are you wasting so much time talking?"

Eight

She had to be dreaming.

That was the only explanation Annie could conceive that would explain her current situation. She hadn't attended a Phillies game in years—not since her husband's death—and even then had always sat in the cheap seats *waaay* up in Veterans Stadium where the atmosphere was thin, and never in a reserved box behind home plate.

There were other similarities, however. The day was hot, the sky as blue as she had ever seen it. Everything else was right, too—the barely restrained roar of the crowd, the aroma of hot pretzels, the warmth of the summer sunshine on the back of her neck making the loose strands of her hair damp and sticky. If she closed her eyes, Annie could almost, *almost,* convince herself that five years had never passed and that she was enjoying a Saturday afternoon ball game with the man she loved.

She opened her eyes. The two males who had accompanied her were as avid fans as Mark had been, and like he, they wore the requisite maroon ball caps and chomped on overpriced, undercooked hot dogs. Mickey also slurped messily on a diluted lemonade while Ike enjoyed a tepid, almost flat beer. They both wore sunglasses, but where Ike's were an expensive pair of Ray•Bans, Mickey's were cheap blue plastic ones decorated with a stegosaurus right between his eyes.

Annie smiled. She supposed nothing had changed after all. She was still enjoying a Saturday afternoon ball game with the men she loved.

Had it been just last night that she and Ike had come together in a frenzy of need and desire? she wondered now. Less than twenty-four hours ago? It didn't seem possible. In spite of their voraciousness, Annie had somehow made it home by two, lingering just inside the front door until considerably later, because Ike took his time when it came to saying—and kissing—good-night. When she had awoke that morning, she had been so certain she must have dreamed the entire episode of the evening before. Making love with him had been too perfect, too unlike anything she had ever experienced. It must have been a fantasy. There was no way it could have been reality.

Then the telephone beside her bed had rung, and a sleep-rusted, very affectionate man's voice had reminded her in vivid detail about all the wondrous activities in which they had indulged. And she'd had to turn her face into the pillow as he'd gone on graphically about the plans he had for her in the future. After that, her body had ached and tingled in all the places he promised to touch again, and she'd realized then that she hadn't dreamed about making love with Ike. She'd realized, too, just how badly she had fallen for him.

Could love possibly happen that quickly? she wondered now. Was love even in fact what she was feeling for him? Or was this rapid reaction simply a case of her body, newly awake for the first time in five years, confusing her mind to think she was in love? She supposed she would simply have to wait to see.

"Strike?" Ike called out angrily at the umpire, snapping Annie out of her reverie.

When he shot up to his feet, Mickey shot up right alongside him.

"Strike?" the little boy mimicked in the same outraged tone of voice.

"How can that be a strike?" Ike demanded, shaking his fist.

Mickey, too, raised a much smaller, tightly clenched hand into the air. "Yeah, how can that be a strike?" he shouted.

Ike expelled a distasteful sound and muttered, "One of these days, ump," as he took his seat again.

"One of these days," Mickey rejoined as he, too, sat down again.

Annie couldn't help but chuckle at the two. The moment they'd entered the stadium, Mickey's jaw had dropped open in wonder, and he'd barely closed it since, mainly because he couldn't stop talking. He asked questions and offered observations about everything, from the personal hygiene habits of the people sitting nearby, to the location of the ice-cream vendor, to the obligatory why is the sky blue and the grass green? And Ike, much to Annie's amazement, had fielded each and every query with the patience and finesse of a man who had been a father for years.

It had been his idea to go to the ball game. He had the use of a friend's box, he'd told Annie on the phone that morning, and although he rarely had the time to take advantage of it, did she know there was a home game today, and did she like baseball, and wouldn't Mickey get a kick out of coming along, too? Annie had replied "Yes" to every question, all the while growing more and more astounded that the man she had come to know as Ike Guthrie was nothing at all like the man she had met at the bachelor auction too long ago to remember.

As the seventh inning drew to a close, Mickey announced, "I hafta go to the bathroom."

"And I think we could use some more hot dogs and pretzels," Ike added. "How about you, Annie?"

She patted her stomach meaningfully. "No thanks. Three of each is my limit. But I'll walk up with you guys. I feel like stretching."

They strode as they had sat, with Mickey between them, and when the crowd threatened to overtake them all, Ike hoisted the little boy up into his arms as if it were the most natural thing in the world to do. Annie watched Mickey's reaction closely. At first, he placed his hands firmly on Ike's shoulders and pushed himself away. When Ike glanced at him curiously, Mickey stilled and studied the big man for a long time. Both of them were still wearing their sunglasses, so Annie couldn't gauge their reactions to each other quite accurately, but she could feel the tension from the little boy gradually rise. She knew he didn't like to have people—particularly people he didn't know well—this close to him. But he seemed to tolerate Ike better than most.

Slowly, little by little, Mickey's anxiousness seemed to abate some. And after another moment of guardedness, he relaxed his arms and allowed Ike to carry him without putting up a fight. He was still wary, Annie noted, but he didn't seem to feel as threatened by Ike as he normally did by grown-ups. Ike couldn't possibly appreciate the significance of Mickey's relatively easy capitulation, she thought. But she was nearly overwhelmed by it.

Evidently she wasn't the only one who was easily succumbing to the lure of Ike Guthrie.

"I'll go ahead and get us a place in the concessions line," she said as the three of them parted ways.

When they joined her again, she noted that Mickey was walking on his own, and Ike had fallen into step behind him, giving the little boy plenty of space. He seemed to realize that he'd inadvertently put Mickey in an uncomfortable situation a moment ago, and was making up for it now by stepping back. Ike was more observant than she'd given him credit for, she realized. But then, why should she be surprised that he would pick up on Mickey's apprehension and be sympathetic to it? He seemed to have been able to read her mind since that first night in Cape May.

When they returned to their box, Mickey ran on ahead of them, hanging over the side of the front rail to get a closer look at the game and offer a more thorough harassment of the umpire. Ike sat himself in the chair beside Annie's that Mickey had previously occupied, then slung his arm over the back of her seat. The warm flesh of his forearm brushed against her shoulders—bare thanks to the thin straps of her army green tank top—and she felt a ripple of pleasure wind through her. When she leaned back, he draped his arm over her shoulders and pulled her close.

"Having fun?" he asked.

She nodded. "I haven't done anything like this in a long time. Too long, in fact."

"I know what you mean. I guess sometimes we get so wrapped up in what we *think* is important that we forget about what *really* is." He was silent for a moment before he added, "I'm sorry about what happened back there."

She glanced over at him, puzzled. "About what?"

"About picking up Mickey that way. It was just an automatic reaction. The kid was about to get trampled. I should have realized it would scare the hell out of him to have somebody big like me scoop him up without warning like that. I'm amazed he didn't go ballistic on me."

She tilted her head to lean it against his shoulder. "Don't beat yourself up about it. Everything turned out fine. And Mickey really likes you."

"Tell me more about him."

The request surprised her. "Mickey?" she asked, just to be sure she understood.

Ike nodded. "You said he was badly mistreated by his parents."

She leaned forward in her seat and turned to face him, pushing her sunglasses up on top of her head. "What they did to him went beyond mistreatment," she said. "They beat him up. Badly. He was only five years old when he came to live with me, but he'd already suffered a number of broken bones, wrenched limbs, smashed fingers..."

Ike grimaced. "I don't think I want to know the details."

"Trust me. I *know* you don't want to know the details."

"But I want to know about him."

Feeling, as usual, overly protective, Annie asked warily, "Why?"

Ike seemed honestly mystified. "I don't know. I just like him. He's a good kid. I can't imagine how he turned out as well as he did, coming from the kind of experience you describe."

Annie relented some. "I think what he has going for him most is that—in spite of being the product of an obviously flawed gene pool—he was born with a good disposition. That and the fact that he's got a couple of good therapists working with him. And he's got a few more people, like me and my staff and the rest of the kids at Homestead, looking out for him."

"A couple of therapists?" Ike repeated.

"It takes a whole bunch of people and a whole lot of time to undo that kind of abuse, Ike. That's why there never seems to be enough money."

He nodded, but she wasn't sure if it was in understanding or not. Finally, he said, "And here I've done nothing but scare the kid more ever since the first day I met him."

"Oh, Ike," she said. She cupped his rough jaw in her palm. "Don't you realize what happened this afternoon when you picked Mickey up?"

"Besides the fact that I terrified him? No."

She shook her head and smiled at his obvious concern. "At first, yes, he was scared. But ultimately he realized what you did was done out of fear for his safety and an honest consideration for him, and not because you intended to harm him. That's a big accomplishment for him. And you helped him achieve it. You did a good thing, Ike."

He covered her hand with his and smiled back. "Really?"

"Really. But I have to admit that I was surprised, too, at first, that he didn't get upset when you picked him up."

"Only at first?"

She nodded. "Then I realized that Mickey just senses exactly what I do about you."

"And what's that?"

She leaned forward and kissed him quickly on the cheek. "That you're a good guy, Ike. I think Mickey just knows that instinctively."

He turned to look at her when she kissed him, but with his eyes hidden by his dark glasses, she had no idea what he had on his mind. Finally, he asked quietly, "You think I'm a good guy?"

"Sure," she replied immediately.

"You didn't always feel that way. Back in Cape May—"

"Back in Cape May I didn't *know* you."

"But now you do?"

She opened her mouth to assure him that after last night, how could she not? Then she felt an odd twinge of uncertainty shimmy down her spine that she couldn't quite shake off. Just because she'd made love to Ike Guthrie didn't mean she knew him, she reminded herself. All things considered, she'd really only met him a matter of weeks ago. And she had been wrong about people before.

In spite of that, she told him, "Of course I do."

Her response seemed to please him, because he smiled. "Good. I was beginning to wonder if you were ever going to come around."

Before she could say more, he gripped her braid in his hand at the base of her nape and held her head in place for a brief, but fierce, kiss. "When can I see you again?"

She chuckled a little nervously. "You're seeing me now."

"You know what I mean." He touched his forehead to hers. "When can I make love to you again?"

"Ike, I—"

"How about tonight?"

Annie groaned inwardly. There was nothing she'd like more. But she wasn't sure if it was a good idea. The feel-

ings he roused in her were too new, too different from anything she'd ever felt before. Even in the early months of her
relationship with Mark, her husband hadn't inspired the
toe-curling, mind-muddling sensations that Ike wreaked in
her with no effort at all.

She needed a little time to make the adjustment. It wasn't
that long ago that she had been completely alone, totally
unconcerned about herself or anything other than her kids.
Now, all of a sudden, Ike was asking her to throw open
wide a part of herself she'd closed off to everyone for years.
Not only that, but he seemed to be inviting himself inside
for a long, long stay. She wasn't sure she was ready for that
just yet. She needed a little time.

"I . . . can't," she told him reluctantly.

"Why not?"

"Because . . ." She sighed fitfully and decided to tell him
the truth. "Because I'm scared, that's why."

He seemed genuinely surprised. "Scared? Still? Of
what?"

"Of what you do to me," she whispered. "It's been a
long time since I've felt like this. Maybe I've never felt quite
like this, I don't know. I'm sorry, but I can't just throw
myself into an affair without a care in the world."

He frowned. "You think that's all this is? An affair?"

"I don't know what it is," she told him honestly. "That's
just the point. And I can't rush into anything until I'm
certain about . . ."

"About what?"

She shrugged, not sure how to tell him what she needed
for him to know. How could she, when she wasn't sure
herself what that was? "Let's just take things one step at a
time, all right?"

He nodded, but she could sense that he wasn't at all
happy about what she'd just revealed. He opened his mouth
to say more—or perhaps to ask her to clarify her fears—but
Mickey rejoined them, carrying an autographed baseball.

"Lookit what the ump just gave me," he said, holding
up his trophy for their inspection.

"Wow," Ike said, sounding suitably impressed. "That's really nice. Not too many people have baseballs autographed by the starting lineup."

"Yeah, he gave it to me, then told me I should bring it up here and show it to my dad." He frowned. "But since ... um ... I don't ..." He broke off with a fitful sigh and grew contemplative. After a moment, he extended the ball toward Ike, his eyebrows arched up in question, his teeth nibbling his lip in worry. "I figured I could just show it to you instead, 'kay?"

Annie watched as Ike's mouth tightened into a thin line, but she could no more tell what he was thinking than she could explain nuclear fusion.

"Yeah, that's fine, sport," Ike told the boy quietly.

He lifted his arm from Annie's shoulder and started to reach out to Mickey. Then he seemed to think better of it, and dropped his hand to his knee.

Mickey looked over his shoulder at the umpire, then back at Ike with an anxious expression. "You don't think the ump gave me this 'cause he was just trying to get rid of me, do you?"

"Nah," Ike assured him immediately. "Who'd want to do a dumb thing like that? You're the best conversationalist I've ever met."

Mickey nodded, seemingly placated, then asked, "Ike?"

"Yeah, sport?"

"What's a confer ... a convo ... a con ..." He sputtered out an exasperated sigh. "What's that?"

Ike smiled and tugged off Mickey's cap, then lightly ruffled his hair. "It means you're my friend," he told the boy.

Mickey smiled. "Yeah?"

Ike nodded. "Yeah."

"Cool."

Ike dropped his arm over Annie's shoulder again and pulled her close once more, then plopped Mickey's cap back on the boy's head, backward. "Yeah," he said quietly. "It is cool."

* * *

Ike couldn't remember the last time he'd been inside a toy store, and he frankly wasn't sure what had led him into this one. He'd only known that one minute, he and Annie and Mickey had been tooling along nicely in his car, and the next, they'd been waltzing through the front door of F.A.O. Schwarz.

Now, as he knelt behind an extremely oversize, bright red Clifford, peeking around the dog's left ear to scope out his territory, he poked another foam dart into his plastic laser rifle and waited. Waited for his quarry—namely Mickey— to show even a hint that he intended to surrender. Waited for just the right opportunity to rain down on the kid's fortress—most recently a scaled-down version of Cinderella's castle on the opposite side of the room.

"He's not going to fall for it," Annie whispered from behind Ike. "He's too smart for that."

"Shh!" Ike commanded. "It'll work. Trust me. He loves the White Ranger best. He told me so."

Between Clifford and Cinderella's castle, stacked very prominently and precariously, was a huge display of the action figure in question. Ike vaguely recalled a time in his life when a comparable exhibit of Scuba G.I. Joe had sent him into a frenzy of delight. No kid could resist such an obvious lure. Any minute now, Mickey would succumb, and then Ike could pick him off like a piece of lint.

"I'm outta here," Annie muttered with a shake of her head. "You guys are impossible. I'll be in the Barbie section, reliving my own childhood. Did you know she has a Ferrari now? Man, that Barbie has *everything*...."

Ike scarcely noted Annie's departure. Instead, he moved to Clifford's tail, snuck a peek first to the left, then to the right, and moved swiftly and silently toward the glass-enclosed cases displaying the Steiff animals. He was amazed to discover that a big hoot owl almost identical to the one his great-aunt Margie had given him for his fifth birthday and that his mother hadn't let him touch until he was eighteen, was commanding three hundred bucks. He was so busy wondering if his mom still had his wrapped in tissue paper in the top of her closet that he didn't hear the rustle of sneakers behind him until it was too late.

"Gotcha."

Ike spun around sharply at the squeaky-voiced announcement, only to find himself cornered by a six-year-old brandishing a neon yellow M-16.

"Raise 'em," Mickey commanded.

Exasperated with himself to no end for getting treed like a cat, Ike slowly lifted his hands into the air, pointing his rifle at the ceiling. "Come on, Mickey," he pleaded, "let's be reasonable about this."

"Give it up, Guthrie," the boy told him. "There's no escape for you now."

Ike thought fast. "Oh, no?"

In a blur of speed, he dropped his rifle and fired the foam dart, hitting Mickey squarely in the knee.

"Aiiieee!" the little boy cried out in mock agony as he dropped to the ground.

But before Ike had a chance to beat a hasty retreat, Mickey rolled onto his side and steadied his M-16, pulling the trigger hard. Ike was pelted with what seemed like hundreds of foam pellets, and he fell to the floor, near death.

"Augh," he cried. "You got me, copper. Everything's going black."

Mickey rose and limped impressively to Ike's side. He held the gun over him as he said, "The state pen's too good for you, you dirty rat. You killed my brother." Then he levered the gun to his shoulder and smiled. "Is that right, Ike? Is that the way I was supposed to say it?"

Ike smiled up at him. "Actually, the dirty rat and brother-killing part was supposed to be my line, but you did it great."

Mickey's smile broadened. "I did?"

Ike nodded. Then he grinned and reached quickly for his laser rifle and pointed it up at Mickey. "Gotcha," he said.

Mickey gaped in disbelief. "Nuh-uh, that's not fair."

"Gotcha," Ike repeated. "You're mine now. You dirty rat. You killed my brother."

And with that, he pulled the trigger. Unfortunately, he was out of ammo. Mickey grinned as he lowered his M-16 once again and aimed it at Ike's heart.

"Okay, you two, that's enough."

Annie stepped up to intercede, collecting their guns as they whined and complained and insisted she couldn't do that without some kind of disarmament treaty, and how come girls never knew how to have fun anyway?

"Girls have plenty of fun," Annie told them. "They just do it a bit more constructively and cooperatively." She shook her head in disgust at the plastic weapons in her hands. "Why on earth, in times like these, do toy manufacturers still make these things?"

Ike jackknifed into a sitting position and absently brushed the foam pellets from his shirt. "Better to have boys play with plastic guns when they're kids and get that kind of aggression out of their systems early," he told her, "than to have them pick up the real things when they're adults."

"Why must they pick them up at all in any version?"

Ike shrugged. "Human nature, Annie. The male animal."

"Animal is right," she muttered.

Ike turned to Mickey. "Did you hear that? She just called us animals."

Mickey's eyebrows shot up in surprise.

Ike nodded. "She did. So let's not disappoint her, okay?"

He rose from the ground, but hunched himself over and dragged his knuckles on the floor, ooh-ooh-oohing and ah-ah-ahing like a chimpanzee. Mickey laughed riotously and immediately joined in the game. All through F.A.O. Schwarz, the two of them played monkey tag, and Annie shook her head in despair. When they made their third pass by her, pretending to pick bananas off her arms to peel and eat them, she sighed.

"When you're ready to go home," she told them, "I'll be waiting in the car."

They swung their arms over their heads, chattered like apes and told her they'd be along shortly.

Nine

"No, no, no, we can't do this. Not here."

Ike glanced over at his partner, hoping the panic that threatened to strangle him wasn't evident in his tone of voice. Unfortunately, Chase Buchanan was looking at him as if he'd just sprouted two more heads, so Ike pretty much figured his alarm was more than evident.

"What do you mean we can't do this?" Chase asked. "This is what we've been doing for more than a year now." He jabbed an index finger down onto a map of Philadelphia, right at the center of a small area highlighted in yellow. "This neighborhood is just ripe for leveling. It's a crime- and vermin-infested area that should have been burned to the ground a decade ago. Soon it will be a public park surrounded by very affordable housing that will be offered for sale to the residents we'll be displacing. We've got all the proper documents and official go-aheads. There's absolutely nothing to keep us from completing this project."

Nothing except for the fact that all of the people in that neighborhood were going to be evicted from their homes, Ike thought, even if they could potentially, *eventually*, wind up in one of the newer, more modern units. Of course, that had already happened nearly a half dozen times, he reminded himself, thanks to his and Chase's beautification contract with the city. And the fact that people had been turned out of their homes by force had never bothered him before.

Before, he'd just shrugged off the realization, and reassured himself that the people being evicted had been bought out of their homes at a price that was more than fair. Then, at worst, they'd all been able to move to other equally depressed neighborhoods that suited their needs just fine. Most of them, however, had ended up in even better dwellings than the ones they'd left behind.

But Ike hadn't cared about any of those people before, because before, none of them had been Annie Malone or her kids.

The yellow area Chase was indicating now was her neighborhood. His partner's index finger had settled within millimeters of the street where she lived. If he had his way, Annie's house would be nothing but a pile of bricks by the end of summer. And Annie and her kids would be... Where? he wondered. As she'd pointed out on a number of occasions, the paltry amount she'd get for her house if she put it up for sale would buy her nothing but another run-down house in another eroding neighborhood, one she'd have to renovate from scratch before the city would allow her kids to enter it.

Which was something that created another problem. Ike and Chase were known for their speed in getting things done. They'd been going into depressed neighborhoods and turning them into everything from shopping centers to public housing, their work generally completed within a matter of months. With all the red tape and politicking that went into the kind of work she did, Annie would need a lot more time than that to resurrect Homestead House.

If she could resurrect Homestead House.

More than likely, Ike thought morosely, she was going to wind up with nothing. No house. No kids. No chance.

"We can't do this," he repeated.

"Why not?" Chase demanded.

"We just...we can't, that's all. If we go in there and level the area, people are going to be displaced from their homes."

Chase scrubbed a hand over his face. "Ike, you're not making sense. Every time we've renovated an area, people have been displaced from their homes. And most of them were glad for the opportunity. The citizens' groups of just about every area we've renovated have welcomed us with open arms."

"*Most* of them," Ike pointed out. "*Just about* every area. Some of the people were resistant."

"But they all still moved into better places, didn't they?" Chase reminded him. "Have we or the city received a single letter of complaint from anyone who wound up in a worse situation than the one they left behind?"

"No."

"Has any aspect of our contract with the city created a negative situation with anyone in any way?"

"No."

"Would we continue doing this kind of thing if we were going to be responsible for anyone winding up on the street?"

Ike brightened. "No. Which is why we can't go into this particular neighborhood. Someone who lives there *will* wind up on the street. Kids. Children, Chase. Children who are already pretty much homeless."

Much to Ike's surprise, his partner nodded. "Homestead House, you mean."

"You know about it?"

Chase waved his hand negligently. "Yeah, but don't sweat it. The city was going to close them down anyway."

This was the first Ike had heard about that. He was certain Annie didn't know, because she would have said something. "What? Why?"

"Because the place is barely up to code, and the neighborhood just isn't what it was ten years ago when the shelter opened. The city has been meaning to get around to closing the house down for a while now, but too many other things have taken precedence. This project is just going to hurry up the inevitable. Those kids would have been displaced anyway. And they'll probably be better off somewhere else."

"Don't count on it," Ike mumbled.

"What?"

"Nothing."

Great. This was just great. Annie was about to lose everything she'd been striving and struggling for ten years to keep together. And Ike was going to be the one holding the cattle prod that hurried the process along.

And just last night, she'd been with him at his place, lying in his arms and gazing at him as if he were the answer to a prayer.

"Who can I talk to about putting this on hold for a while?" he asked.

Chase shook his head, confused. "No one. I already told you—the project's a go. The area has been declared blighted, and the city has already sent out letters of intent to all the residents of the neighborhood. They'll be arriving in today's mail."

Ike clenched his fists helplessly, wanting to hit something. Hard. "Why wasn't I kept better informed about this?"

Chase glared at him. "You were. You initialed your okay on the memo about the new project a month ago, and you co-signed the proposal we sent to the city weeks ago."

"I did?"

"Yes, you did. Then you abruptly took more than a week of vacation time and didn't call the office once."

"I didn't?"

"No, you didn't." Chase eyed him thoughtfully. "Frankly, I was starting to get a little concerned about that. You've been acting awfully funny lately." He smiled. "Ever since you came back from Cape May with your new owner, now that I think about it. You know, Sylvie always said all it was going to take was the right woman to bring you to your senses. Is that what's been going on for the past month? You're finally coming to your senses?"

Ike dropped his head into his hands and sighed heavily. Was there anything in the world that could make this day worse than it already was? He couldn't imagine a single thing. "Oh, yeah. I'm coming to my senses all right. And they're telling me I'm in *biiig* trouble. As a matter of fact—"

The intercom on his desk buzzed loudly, and before he could even respond, his secretary's voice followed, sounding more than a little alarmed. "Mr. Guthrie, Mr. Buchanan, I think you should come out here right away."

Ike and Chase exchanged wary glances, then headed for the door. On the other side, their handful of office workers stood in the reception area, gazing nervously first at their bosses, then in the direction of the elevators, an area Ike couldn't see from where he currently stood. A buzz of conversation halted from the small circle of employees, then was replaced by louder voices in the distance and the eruption of white lights, some bursting like the flashbulbs on cameras, some steadily lit like those mounted on video recorders.

A sense of dread and foreboding settled over Ike. Slowly, cautiously, knowing instinctively that he wasn't going to like what he saw, he moved to join his office workers with Chase right behind him. When he finally saw what they saw, he closed his eyes tight, and realized at once that there was in fact one thing that could make the day worse than it already was.

Annie Malone had chained herself to the front door of their office. And she'd had the foresight to alert the media ahead of time.

At the moment, she was giving them an impassioned account of the history of Homestead House. That, he was certain, would be followed by an even more impassioned condemnation of Buchanan-Guthrie Designs, Inc., the big corporation that would be turning helpless children out onto the streets of Philadelphia to fend for themselves. She sat on the floor in a wispy white dress and sandals, her legs and arms bare. Her hair was gathered loosely at her nape with a piece of twine, and she wore no other decoration.

Oh, she was good, he thought. A real pro. She looked sweet, innocent, virginal...just ripe for being victimized by callous businessmen and politicians. She had the face and voice of an angel. He was going to come off looking like the very devil when he challenged her.

"What the hell...?" Chase began.

"You better let me handle this," Ike told him. He settled a hand on his secretary's shoulder and turned her toward her desk as he passed. "Call maintenance and see if they can send someone up with a pair of bolt cutters." As an afterthought, he added, "And you better call security, too."

The moment he began to approach the scene, the newspeople turned their attention to him. There was a representative from every local station, he noted, and at least one network. Annie must have been on the phone all morning to get that kind of reaction. Just what time did she get her mail?

Stay calm, he instructed himself as the journalists began to fire one question after another at him. *Ignore the inquisition, but don't look like a jerk. That's exactly what these people want.*

As much as Ike cared for Annie, he refused to elevate her to the status of martyr. Especially when he would wind up being the one responsible for her crucifixion. So he tried to look as harmless as possible as he drew near.

"Annie," he said softly, dropping to rest his weight on his haunches beside her. "What do you think you're...?"

He was struck further speechless when her gaze met his. When he'd taken her home the night before, her eyes had been lit with warmth and laughter and affection. Now they were shuttered and empty and cold.

"You bastard," she said levelly. Her voice was too quiet for anyone but him to hear. "You coldhearted, lying, manipulative, sonofa—"

"Watch it."

His voice had dropped as low as hers, so the ever-resourceful media members thrust their microphones lower, right into Ike's and Annie's faces.

"Mr. Guthrie, aren't you and your partner responsible for the evictions of thousands of Philadelphia residents?"

"Ms. Malone, care to comment on the mayor's claim that you're a militant subversive?"

"Mr. Guthrie, is it true that you hate children?"

"Ms. Malone, aren't you the same woman whose husband was killed five years ago trying to save one of your children's lives?"

Both Annie and Ike glared at the reporter who posed the final question.

"Don't you people have something constructive to do with your lives?" he demanded. "My God, isn't there any *real* news happening in the world? There's got to be a war breaking out somewhere that's infinitely more significant than the little drama Ms. Malone is playing out for you here."

"'Little drama?'" Annie hissed indignantly. "Well, that's pretty typical of the mentality of corporate America, isn't it?"

Ike returned his attention to Annie. "And just what, pray tell, do you consider the mentality of corporate America, Ms. Malone?"

"Shortsighted moneygrubbing, Mr. Guthrie. *That's* the mentality of corporate America."

"I see."

"What you see is dollar signs, nothing more."

"What I see is an opportunity to replace a dangerous, crime-ridden neighborhood with an area that has substantially more opportunity."

"More opportunity for big business, you mean."

"More opportunity for the citizens of Philadelphia."

"You don't think I'm stupid or naive enough to—"

"What I think, Ms. Malone," Ike interrupted her, quickly nearing the end of his patience, "is that you'd be better off if you stopped behaving like a little girl and started acting like a woman." This had gone on long enough, Ike thought. And he knew exactly what to say to put an end to it. "The way you've been acting like a woman with me at night."

He was completely unprepared for the sharp sting of Annie's palm striking his cheek. He'd had no idea the flat of a woman's hand could hurt like that. Then again, he supposed if she'd been another woman, the pain wouldn't have been nearly as severe. Ike rubbed his cheek thoughtfully and touched his tongue to the corner of his mouth. But he said nothing to comment on her action.

The members of the media were silenced for a moment by their exchange. Then they chorused as one, "At night?"

Annie snapped her mouth shut, and narrowed her eyes at him. Her cheeks were stained with red, a flush that swept downward to disappear into her neckline. Oh, boy, was she mad, Ike thought. Maybe he should have kept his own mouth shut.

"Ms. Malone," the man holding the largest microphone interjected, "are you and Mr. Guthrie involved in a romantic relationship?"

She hesitated for a moment before she replied, "Oh, I wouldn't call what we have *romantic*." Her voice was surprisingly well modulated, something that troubled Ike greatly for some reason. He realized why when she added, "He and his company will be lucky if I don't slap them with a lawsuit."

"*What?*" Ike cried. "What the hell are you talking about?"

He felt a hand clamp over his shoulder and looked up to find Chase staring down at him. "Maybe you better let *me* handle this," his partner suggested.

Ike nodded and stood. As loudly and clearly as he dared, he said, "Oh, Chase, by the way, this is Annie Malone. My new owner. The woman who spent the weekend in Cape May with me, and who's made me come to my senses. Annie, this is my partner, Chase. You two should get along real well. You both think I'm a jackass."

He started to walk away, but hesitated. "Then again," he added, "at the moment, I can't disagree with you on that account." His next words were spoken to Chase, but offered for Annie's consumption. "Tell security I want to see her before they take her down to the police station."

Annie gasped. "The police station?"

He eyed her levelly. "Yeah, sweetheart, the police station. You're trespassing, you've slandered me, you've threatened me and you've assaulted me. I don't know what kind of upbringing you had, but where I come from, that's not very nice. It's also not very legal."

And with that, Ike turned away again and headed back to his office. If he was generous with himself, he figured he had about ten minutes to figure out what the hell he was going to do.

Annie couldn't remember when she'd ever been more furious. Had it really only been hours since she'd waken up in a house full of sunshine and exuberant children, feeling as if nothing in her life would ever go wrong again? She'd hugged the kids as she had done every morning, had bantered with Nancy and Jamal about their studies as she normally did, had made her usual to-do and shopping lists. Then she'd picked up the mail.

The official-looking envelope from the city had been the first thing to catch her eye. The letter enclosed inside it had been what actually shook her to her core. It had been more than a little troubling to discover that she was about to lose Homestead House, something that meant more to her than just about anything in the world. But it had been devastating to discover that Ike, the one thing that did matter most, was one of the people responsible for taking it away from her.

And now she stood face-to-face with her nemesis between two big rent-a-cops who gripped her upper arms with bruising strength. Ike sat on the other side of the room behind a big, mahogany desk, his jacket off, his necktie askew, his sleeves rolled to his elbows, his head rested in his hands. She couldn't see his face, but just from observing his posture, Annie thought he looked tired. Which was good, she decided. That would make it much easier for her to strangle the life out of him.

As if he'd detected her thoughts, his head snapped up to look at her, and he frowned at the two security guards restraining her.

"Let go of her," he told them, speaking to them as if they were children. "She's not an assassin, for God's sake."

The two men exchanged looks over the top of Annie's head, then glanced back at Ike, as if questioning the wisdom of his command.

"Let her go," he repeated more forcefully, rising to his full height, which was considerably taller than either of theirs. "Now."

The two men released her at once.

"And get out."

"But, Mr. Guthrie—" one of the men objected.

"Get . . . out."

The two men looked at each other again, shook their heads as if certain Ike were an idiot who was about to die a slow and horrible death—something Annie knew wasn't too far off the mark, if she had her way—then exited without further resistance. Ike watched them go until the door swung closed behind them, mumbling something under his breath about speaking to the building manager about hiring a different security company, pronto. Then he looked at her again.

"I'm sorry, Annie," he said softly. He shoved his hands into his trouser pockets and walked casually to the front of his desk, leaning back against it. "Did they hurt you?"

She frowned at him. "Those two goons? No, *they* didn't hurt me. Anything else you want to know before you call the Black Shirts come to get me, *Il Duce?*"

Ike sighed. Annie didn't think she'd ever seen him looking this tired.

"Yeah," he told her, "one or two things."

She studied her nails and said, "Shoot."

"First I want you to know something. I had no idea your neighborhood was one of the ones we were going to be..."

"Razing?" she suggested.

"Renovating," he countered.

She dropped her hand to her side and stared at him. "Don't lie to me anymore, Ike. I think you've done enough of that already."

"I've never lied to you."

She expelled a derisive sound. "You're nothing but a lie."

"Annie—"

"Suddenly, it all makes sense. Why you've kept after me to move my kids somewhere else. Why you've badgered me about what a dangerous place I was living in. Why you ever showed up at my house to begin with..."

"Why I helped you fix the place up?" he added. "Yeah, that made real sense, didn't it? I sweated my ass off to practically rebuild your house just so it could be torn down again."

Annie frowned at him.

"Think about it, Annie."

"Don't you think I have been? All morning long, all I've done is try to figure out how you could do something like this." She took a few steps forward, became exhausted by the simple action, and dropped onto the sofa along the wall. She tipped her head back to look at the ceiling and sighed. "I would have sworn on my life that you genuinely cared about us—all of us."

"I do care about you. I—"

"And Mickey," she went on without acknowledging his assurance. "Okay, even though it hurts to admit it, I can see how you could double-cross me, because I'm an adult. I have the maturity and capacity to deal with betrayal. For the most part."

"I haven't betrayed anyone. I've never—"

"But Mickey's just a child. A child." She brought her head forward again to meet his gaze levelly. "And he loves you, Ike. He's told me he loves you. Do you realize how important that is? Do you fully understand what it means for a child like him, who's suffered so much abuse, to open himself up enough to actually admit that he cares for someone? Can it penetrate that thick skull of yours or that thick shell of ice surrounding your heart just what this is going to do to him?"

"Don't you dare accuse me of betraying anyone. Not you. And not..." He pushed himself away from his desk and began to pace like a caged animal. "And not Mickey. I'd never do anything to hurt that kid." He spun quickly around and pinned her in place with his gaze. "And I'd never do anything to hurt you."

She almost believed him. God help her, she almost let herself accept what he said as true. Then she remembered the photostat copy of a letter that had accompanied the one from the city, and Ike Guthrie's scrawled signature at the bottom of it. He'd okayed the entire project in that letter, and it had been dated two days before he'd started sniffing around her front door.

"You've already hurt me," she said softly. "You've hurt everyone at Homestead. Eventually, I'll get over it. But the kids won't. You're just one more bad thing that's happened to them in their lives. They'll see you as verification that they can't trust anyone. But something tells me you're not going to lose any sleep over it."

He turned his back to her and stared out the window at the Philadelphia skyline. "I'm going to lose more than sleep," he said softly. "A lot more."

Annie forced herself not to care about the fact that he seemed genuinely distressed. He was a good actor, she reminded herself. He'd actually had her convinced that she meant something to him. She'd even begun to indulge in silly little fantasies about the three of them—herself and Ike and Mickey—living together as a family should. Ever since she'd met the little boy, she'd wanted to adopt Mickey as her own. But she'd been assured that as a single woman, she didn't stand a chance. With Ike by her side, she'd begun to think—even if only casually for now—that maybe someday the two of them could claim Mickey as their son.

Boy, had she been snowed.

"Are you going to have me arrested or what?" she finally asked. She wanted to be out of Ike's office, out of his life. And if that meant leaving in handcuffs, at least she'd be rid of him.

"No, I'm not going to have you arrested," he said without turning around. "Are you going to sue me?"

Annie thought for a moment, then said, "I haven't decided yet."

"Well, let me know when you figure it out."

Figure it out, she repeated to herself. That was a good one. "Yeah, I'll be in touch," she finally told him.

"I don't doubt that for a moment."

She strode silently to the door, gripped the knob, and started to pull it open.

"Annie?"

She pivoted slowly around to find Ike still staring out the window. "Yes?"

"Did Mickey really tell you he loved me?"

She hesitated only a moment before telling him, "Yes. He did. While I was tucking him in Saturday night. He was holding on to that stuffed owl you bought him like it was the Holy Grail. And right after I turned off the light, he told me he loved you." She rubbed at the tears stinging her eyes and added, "He's never said that about anyone, Ike. Not even me."

Ike nodded almost imperceptibly, but said nothing more. So Annie opened the door and walked out of his office and tried to forget about the way her heart seemed to have stopped beating. Instead, she tried to focus all her mental energy on working out a way to keep Homestead House alive.

Ten

Four thousand, eight hundred and seventy-seven dollars and fifty-three cents. That's how much money was left in the Homestead House bank account. Annie rubbed her eyes wearily with the thumb and index finger of one hand, and twirled a pencil restlessly between the fingers of the other. For a few idle moments, she wondered how difficult it might be to knock off an armored car. Then she mentally tallied the number of days before Publisher's Clearing House had their next sweepstakes drawing, and regretted not having subscribed to at least one of their magazines. Maybe if she bought a couple of lottery tickets...

She sighed and tossed her pencil onto the pile of bank statements, then stretched her arm out flat on her desk and bent to settle her forehead against it. It wasn't her quickly dwindling bank account that was troubling her most right now, she knew. It was Ike Guthrie's betrayal.

She still hadn't quite gotten over what had happened, still hadn't quite come to terms with the fact that she had been so thoroughly duped. A full week had passed since she'd walked out of his office and his life without a backward glance. She had spent nearly every waking moment since then talking on the phone or knocking on doors or meeting with whomever would listen to her complaints and fears. She had done everything within her power and knowledge to prevent Homestead House from becoming another casualty of urban renewal. And she had failed to win even the tiniest reprieve.

What made matters worse was that deep down, she knew what she was struggling to keep alive had been a dying beast for a long time. Homestead House had been iffy since the day she and Mark had opened its doors. In the back of her mind, she'd known for years that the day would come when she'd be shut down, either because she ran out of money, or because the house and neighborhood had simply become unsafe. She tried to find reassurance in the knowledge that what was happening now was something that should have happened years ago, and she told herself she should be grateful for what little extra time she'd been granted.

Unfortunately, Annie could find no reassurance at all. And she didn't want to go down without a fight. She couldn't let her kids—her family—be disbanded by the stroke of a pen and at the whim of a government. She refused to let a couple of overpaid pin-striped executives and a handful of underpaid city officials dictate the worth of her home and her life's work. She would not, not as long as she was capable of drawing breath, allow her kids to wind up in situations that could be potentially worse than the ones that had landed them in Homestead House to begin with.

And, dammit, she would not let a two-faced, opportunistic user like Ike Guthrie be the one to bring them down.

Nevertheless, Annie had no idea how to proceed. She'd never felt so helpless in her life. She had no one to turn to, no one who could—or would—offer to help her out. In her desperation, she'd even turned to her sister for help. But all

Sophie had done was reiterate that it was time for Annie to come to her senses and be realistic. It was time she saw just how pointless it was even to try to change the world. Life was unfair, Sophie had told her. Annie might just as well get used to it. And, by the way, her sister had wondered, how were things going with that nice architect she'd bought for her?

Annie knew better than nearly anyone about life's injustices—she had, after all, seen the victims of such unfairness over and over again. And being the witness to such things only made her that much more determined to fight back.

She straightened in her chair, picked up her pencil and jammed it between her teeth, biting down until she could taste the lead at its center. Then she spun around in her chair and wheeled herself over toward the filing cabinet. There had to be someone, she thought. Somewhere. Someone out there besides her must care enough about these kids to keep them from being lost in the system forever.

Immediately, Ike's face swam up from the dark recesses of her brain, as if taunting her. She grunted noncommittally as she pushed the thought away and tried to focus on her files. Oh, yeah, he cared, she thought. Cared about all the great money he and his partner were going to make after razing her house and building a co-op in its place. Cared about the nice little sexual diversion she'd offered him while he was busy casing the joint. Cared about how easy it had been to pluck her right off the vine like the stupid sap she was.

And here she had fancied herself in love with him.

Annie expelled a derisive sound and pushed her bangs away from her face, telling herself she would not cry. Instead, she pulled a file from the drawer, thinking maybe the Dobbins Corporation, who had been regular contributor to Homestead House years ago—before they had filed for chapter eleven—might have gotten back on their feet financially again by now.

The front doorbell rang then, stilling her fingers on the telephone buttons before she had the chance to make the call. Even though she knew Nancy or one of the kids would respond, Annie sat silently and waited, knowing somehow that whoever had come calling had come for a reason other than a social visit. Although she hadn't yet told the kids about what was going to happen to Homestead House, she knew they were smart enough to know something was wrong. There had been an uneasy quiet in the house for the past week, as if everyone were fearful and edgy.

Annie, too, had felt that way. She felt that way, right now, in fact. And when Nancy appeared at her office door with a big man looming behind her, Annie immediately understood why.

"Annie," Nancy said quietly, as if she, too, felt the uncomfortable tension that seemed to erupt in the room, "you, uh, you have a visitor."

"Thanks, Nancy."

The young woman left quickly, looking over her shoulder at Ike as she went. He was dressed not in his work-on-the-house uniform of grubby jeans and T-shirt that she had become accustomed to see him wearing when he came by, but in the trappings of his true self—a power suit and silk tie, and shiny black shoes that had probably cost him more than she spent in a week on groceries for a houseful of children. She told herself she was relieved to see him dressed this way. It would remind her of who she was actually dealing with.

A shark. A cold-blooded, ruthless, single-minded animal who thought of nothing but consuming whatever crossed his path.

"You're not welcome here," she told him, hoping her voice sounded steadier than her nerves felt. "For the time being, this is still my house. And you aren't welcome here."

She wasn't sure, but she thought he actually winced at her declaration. Nevertheless, he took a few steps into her office and told her, "I've come on official business."

She stood, knowing she was going to have enough trouble handling him without being seated in a submissive position. "Of course it's official. What other business would you have here? What other business *is* there for you, other than the official? Certainly not social. Or personal. Or—"

"Official," he repeated, clearly growing impatient. "Now if you wouldn't mind, there are a couple of things we need to discuss."

Annie swept her arm toward the chair on the other side of her desk, but Ike didn't kid himself for a moment that the gesture was gracious or inviting in any way. She looked like hell, he thought as he moved to take the seat she indicated. Her eyes were smudged with dark circles, and her cheeks seemed a bit hollow, as if she hadn't eaten a bite in the week since he'd last seen her. Her loose khaki trousers obviously hadn't been ironed, and her white, short-sleeved shirt, half spilling from her waistband and not all the way buttoned, sported a couple of stains. Her hair was wound loosely atop her head, held in place by some invisible means and lacking the shine and luster it normally held.

She looked tired and frail and desperate. And he knew he was the cause of that.

No sooner had he taken his seat than she demanded, "What do you want?"

He reached inside his jacket pocket and extracted a thin white envelope. "To give you this."

She took it from him gingerly, dangling it between thumb and forefinger, careful not to make any physical contact with him when she did so. Her gaze never left his as she ran her thumb under the seal, then withdrew and unfolded a crisp sheet of white linen paper. Quickly, she scanned the message, then looked up at him again.

"You could have just mailed this," she said. "There was no reason for you to come all the way down here."

"I wanted to make sure you got it."

"Then you could have just sent some government lackey to bring it."

"I wanted to bring it myself."

"Why?"

"Just to be sure."

"But why?" she asked again. Without looking back, she tossed the missive onto her cluttered desk. "Why is it so damned important that I get this letter? It just reiterates everything I already knew. You've had the neighborhood declared blighted so you can come in and raze a twelve-block area, taking away everyone's house, including *my* house. You're evicting me and my kids from our home so you can build a nice, new, structurally sound, yuppie magnet in its place. So what?"

He frowned at her. "The only thing I'm guilty of in that string of charges is that I am in fact the one who's designed the new buildings around here. Other than that, you have no right to charge me with anything. I am *not* the one evicting you from your home."

"You might as well be."

"But I'm not."

"Okay, I stand corrected. So, what else is it so important for me to know?"

Ike expelled an impatient sound. She just wasn't going to give him an inch, was she? Then again, he asked himself, had he really expected her to?

"That letter also states," he continued restlessly, "that you're going to be receiving nearly three times what you paid for this house to begin with. It will be more than enough for a down payment on a new place for you and the kids. This place. You could move into the new building that's going to be here, Annie. It doesn't have to be a co-op. It could be a nice townhouse. And it could be yours. Nothing would have to change at all."

She leaned back against her desk, crossed her arms over her midsection, and smiled. But the expression was in no way happy. "Yeah, right. Think about that for a minute, Ike. In the first place, I need to buy a house I can pay for in full up front, because there's never going to be any guarantee of a steady income for mortgage payments."

"But—"

"In the second place, where are the kids and I supposed to stay while this brave new world is being built? Even if by some wild miracle we do manage to find a temporary shelter, once this neighborhood is all renewed and revamped, do you honestly think the new tenants are going to welcome us back with open arms?"

He gritted his teeth. "Why wouldn't they?"

She expelled a single, humorless chuckle. "A halfway house for troubled kids? Kids who will remind them every day of their lives that there's a big bad world out there they'd rather not know about? Kids they'd rather see locked up somewhere nice and safe and completely out of even their most peripheral vision?

"This is going to be a bright new neighborhood filled with optimism and opportunity. Nobody living here is going to want any kind of blemish like us spoiling that image. And it's going to be the same in any neighborhood we approach. By the time I manage to find a suitable site for Homestead House—*if* I manage to find one—my kids are going to be disbursed all over the place. And the chances are good that any progress I've managed to make with them will be completely undone."

Ike wished he could deny her assertion, but knew that what she said was probably true. "Well, at least you're willing to admit that there will be some opportunity here."

"Oh, sure, I'll admit that," she replied. "There will be plenty of opportunity. For other people. Not for us."

"Annie—"

"We have nowhere to go, Ike. The people around here tolerate us now because we've been a part of the neighborhood for a long time, and we blend in nicely with the scenery. Everything around here is pretty much damaged and misbegotten, including the residents of Homestead House. But once this neighborhood is all fixed up, nice and shiny and new, no one is going to accept us. No one."

He balked at the certainty in her voice. "There must be some alternative. It can't possibly be as bad as you make it out to be."

She pushed herself away from her desk and took a couple of steps toward him, then, as if she thought better of it, stopped right where she stood. "I seem to recall you yourself saying not so long ago, back when you were disparaging my life-style, that...let me think now...how exactly did you put it?" She pressed her fingers to her forehead, as if struggling to retrieve a not-so-deeply buried memory. "Oh, yeah, now I remember. You said, 'The Age of Aquarius ended twenty-five years ago. People found out they couldn't change the world with love-ins and protests. Nobody cared then. Nobody cares now. Deal with it.'"

She crossed her arms over her chest again and frowned. "I do deal with it, Ike. Every single day. I know no one cares. Nothing has been made more clear to me than that over the past few days. But that doesn't mean *I'm* going to stop caring."

Ike wished he would choke on the words she'd thrown back at him. Then he wouldn't have to stand here seeing her look so defeated and betrayed, and knowing he was responsible for it.

"I've called everyone I know," she went on when he said nothing to defend himself. "I've tried cajoling, bribing, threatening, begging.... Still, everyone has a handy excuse or reason why they can't help me out." She met his gaze levelly and unflinchingly. "But it's not over yet. Even though Homestead House has had a good run, probably longer than it deserved, I won't roll over until the last gasp of breath leaves my lungs."

Instinctively, Ike wanted to reach out to her, but he stopped himself just short of completing the gesture. Halfheartedly, he said, "You can't fight City Hall."

She returned to her desk and slumped into her chair, propping her elbows on her desk, resting her forehead in her hands. "Maybe not. I'm tired, and at the moment, I feel like I've been beaten to a bloody pulp." When she lifted her head to look at him, her eyes were bright with unshed tears. "But I won't give up. I can't, Ike. I can't."

Ike stared at her dismally. It was pointless for her to go on. She was never going to win. Everyone and everything was against her. Every other family in the neighborhood was tickled pink to be receiving such a large sum of money for a home they'd come to think of as nearly worthless. Everyone else in the neighborhood was already packing and shopping around for a new home. Everyone else was behind this project one hundred percent. Because everyone else had absolutely nothing to lose and everything to gain.

But Annie was going to lose everything.

Deep down, Ike had known all along that she would dig in and fight with every last breath to keep Homestead House open and right where it was. And, if he was honest with himself, he knew he didn't want her to give up. He had hoped she *would* fight with him. In spite of everything, he was glad to know she would be defiant to the end, would challenge to the fullest of her ability every intention the city and his company professed to have toward her house. He looked forward to her annoying the hell out of all of them, and making his working environment impossible. He hadn't expected to see her easily defeated.

But what she was proposing to do was futile. And, with the sentiment in the neighborhood being what it was, it could be potentially dangerous. If her efforts to save Homestead House wound up prolonging the checks due to the other members of the community for their homes, the other members of the community might just lose their already tenuous tolerance for Annie and her kids. And people did crazy things when money was involved.

"We'll have this house eventually," Ike told her. "Deep down, you know that as well as I do."

He wasn't sure, but he thought she nodded her head. Still, she said nothing.

"And when that happens, where will you go?" he asked. "Where will the kids go?"

She lifted one shoulder in a halfhearted shrug. "I'll manage somehow. I've been offered a couple of jobs over the years, but I always turned them down because Homestead was so much more important to me. I can make a few calls. If it becomes necessary, I'll find something.''

"But the kids?" Ike asked, wondering why she was avoiding a subject he knew was much closer to her heart than her own welfare would ever be. "What about them?"

She dropped her gaze to study the floor. "If something happens to Homestead House, they'll wind up in public facilities or foster care. Places where people are paid to watch them, but couldn't care less for their welfare otherwise.''

She snapped up her head to eye him again. "But, hey, don't worry yourself about it, Ike. They'll thrive in situations like that. They'll just *thrive*. They might even learn a trade or two to help carry them through life. Like burglary, for example. Or car-jacking. Or assault. Even a little guy like Mickey can master those skills real quick. Especially once he's surrounded again by people who don't give a damn about him.''

Even without her sarcastic tone of voice punctuating the statement, Ike knew as well as Annie that *fine* was the last thing her kids were going to be without her influence in their lives. But, dammit, there was nothing he could do about that now. If it was within his power, he'd invite them all to stay at his place until everything could be straightened out. But he had neither the room, nor the financial means to take care of such a crowd. Yeah, he was wealthy, he reminded himself. But even the Rockefellers didn't have ready cash like that.

"There's got to be something we can do," he told her.

"We?" she repeated. "How dare you suggest you have a stake in this after you—"

"Annie, I swear to you, if I had known your neighborhood was—"

"Quit lying to me!"

The words exploded from her mouth as if they'd been launched from her lungs with a catapult, so loud and venomous, it startled them both. Annie dropped her head to avoid looking at Ike, and he glanced away, wishing that things could be different.

"I didn't know," he insisted quietly. "I swear to you, Annie. I didn't know your neighborhood was next. I never would have okayed the project if I had. And I certainly would have warned you, and given you as much time as you needed to make arrangements for your kids."

"Your signature on the prospectus says differently. It clearly indicates that my neighborhood was next on the docket. And it was dated two days before you started coming to Homestead House."

"And nearly three weeks after I met you," he pointed out. "I didn't even realize what I was signing when I put my name on that thing."

"Didn't you?" Her voice was doubtful.

"No. By God, Annie, you've had me tied in knots since the day I met you. It's amazing I actually *could* sign my name on something, when half the time, I can't even remember what it is."

"Don't," she told him. "Don't even start. I won't be taken in by that again."

"By what?"

"By your flattery and cajoling." Slowly, she shook her head, as if she were considering something for the first time. "I knew it was ridiculous for me to think a man like you could be interested in me. You're too handsome and successful, and I'm too nondescript. But all along, I let myself be sucked further and further along by your sweet talk. And all along, it was nothing but lip service."

It was the wrong phrase to use, and they both recognized that immediately. Ike's gaze flew to Annie's mouth, and he parted his own lips helplessly as he remembered what it had been like to join his mouth to hers. In a single, swift flash, he recalled every moment of the incredible lovemaking they'd enjoyed together, remembered the soft swell of her breasts pressing into his chest, the taut smoothness of her belly beneath his fingertips, the firm warmth of her thighs gliding alongside his. He thought again about the sounds she'd uttered when he'd touched her just so, recalled the way she'd smelled, the way she'd tasted, the way she'd shuddered around him at the culmination of their union.

"Annie," he whispered as he rose from his seat and closed the distance between them in three easy strides. Almost as if he had no control over himself, he pulled her into his arms, and she fell against him, limp. "Don't do this to us. Please."

She turned her head just the slightest bit, as if she were silently asking him to kiss her. But when he bent his head forward to do just that, she pushed him fiercely away.

"Get out of my house," she told him, her words quiet and firm and edged with bitterness. "Now."

"Annie, don't—"

"Now."

Ike flexed his fingers savagely before doubling his hands into fists, feeling angrier and more helpless than he'd ever felt in his life. He crossed the room silently, but lingered by the door for a moment. Unable to help himself, he turned to look at Annie one final time. She still stood behind her desk, her head bowed, her forehead cupped by her palm, her entire body slumped forward in defeat.

"They were going to shut you down anyway, you know," he told her.

She nodded, but didn't look at him. "Yeah, I know. *They* were going to shut me down. In the long run, I think I could have handled that." She, too, straightened, and turned to face him fully. "But it's *you* who's closing me down now, Ike. You. Think about that when you're standing in the middle of your beautiful urban renewal. And try to forget you ever set foot in Homestead House. I know I'm going to try my damnedest to do just that."

"Think you can?"

She sighed and turned away again. "Guess I'll have the rest of my life to find out, won't I?"

* * *

Annie wasn't sure what woke her. When she opened her eyes, her room was dark, and the only sounds present were those to which she had long ago become accustomed and which she generally ignored in sleep—the irregular whir of the portable fan sitting in front of her open window, the steady buzz of the street lamp outside, the occasional shouts of the teenagers who congregated on the corner in the street below her window. Nothing unusual. A typical hot summer night. So what had woken her?

She sat up in bed and pushed her hair out of her eyes, then cocked her head to the side to listen. But she heard nothing out of the ordinary. Nevertheless, an odd suspicion wound through her, telling her there was in fact something wrong.

Annie could have shrugged off the sensation as simple sleep-induced paranoia, nothing more than the leftover remnants of an unremembered dream. But some strange things had been happening around Homestead House in the last couple of weeks—ever since she'd initiated an action to sue the city of Philadelphia and Buchanan-Guthrie Designs, Inc. and had won a restraining order against both.

She didn't for a moment kid herself that she was going to win either lawsuit. She was paying a lawyer virtually every dime she had left to have him tell her just that. But until she had her day in court, the suits held up any progress toward the razing and renovation of her home and her neighborhood. They bought her a little time. Unfortunately, they also held up any financial remuneration that everyone else in the area was due and expecting for the sale of a crumbling home.

It had made some of Annie's neighbors a bit angry. It had made others absolutely venomous.

And strange things had begun to occur as a result, things that prohibited her from shrugging off even the tiniest fear of danger. She'd been getting hate mail on a regular basis, along with telephoned threats. All anonymous, of course. And rough, resentful spray-painted messages had appeared on the exterior walls of Homestead House. Messages that said things like, "Get out while U can" and "Cut it out now" and others that were too troubling to recall.

So Annie sat up in bed and listened harder, hoping to discern what exactly was different about this night than any other, trying to figure out why she should feel so threatened. Her heart pumped a little more furiously than usual, her breathing became a bit more shallow. Yet her ears picked up nothing other than the normal night sounds of the city. Nevertheless, she stood, padded barefoot to her closet, and threw a ragged terry cloth bathrobe on over her T-shirt and boxer shorts. Then she moved as quietly as she could to her bedroom door and eased it open.

The hallway was darker than her room, the only light present a weak shaft of hazy bluish white, thrown up over the stairwell from the fluorescent light above the sink in the kitchen below. Still she heard nothing. But something was wrong. She knew it immediately. A woman living alone in the heart of the inner city learned fast to hone her instincts. And over the years, Annie's had become unimpeachable. If she sensed danger, it was there.

She looked first to her left, then to her right, half expecting some odious shape to spring at her out of the darkness. But only more silence greeted her. There were four rooms on the second floor of Homestead House—Annie's and those assigned to the youngest of the children—while the teenagers shared three rooms on the third floor. She was about to head upstairs, thinking the older kids more likely to be awake and causing trouble, then halted when she heard something from the living room below.

A splash. A soft, quick splash of liquid that was followed by another. And then another. And another.

Someone was in her house. Someone who didn't belong there. Her first reaction was to retreat to her bedroom, to dial 911 and cower under the covers until the police arrived. Then the acrid smell of gasoline made her nostrils twitch, and she realized that whoever was downstairs had every intention of burning down her house. That faceless, silent somebody had only to scratch a match against the wall, and Homestead House—and all its occupants—would go out in a blaze of glory.

Like hell we will.

The words erupted in Annie's brain as she made her way quietly toward the stairs. She leaned over the banister and squinted into the living room, seeing two dark and very large shapes making their way easily around the perimeter of the room, tossing gasoline against the walls as they went. One man mumbled something to the other, and the second man chuckled low. It was an awful, menacing sound, and it made Annie mad. Try to burn her out, would they? Maybe in another life. Not in this one.

The only weapons Annie kept in the house were those whose primary roles had nothing to do with inflicting injury on other people. Kitchen knives, for example. And heavy wrenches. And baseball bats. Like the one she kept under her bed. Silently, she crept back to her bedroom to retrieve it, then glanced longingly at the telephone. 911 was only three quick punches, she told herself. How long could that possibly take?

She snatched up the receiver, only to find that the phone was dead. No accident, she was sure. Dropping the receiver onto the bed, she clenched the bat with two strong fists and headed out again. She hugged the wall as she made her way down the stairs, knowing they were less likely to squeak there, thankful in the back of her mind to Ike, who had done such a good job reinforcing them, nearly silencing completely their old creaking.

The two men had moved beyond the living room to the dining room, where they continued their labor, streaking the walls with gasoline. Annie wasn't sure what kind of chance she stood with one ash baseball bat against two big men. So she forced herself not to think about it. Maybe if she startled them, she'd scare them away. At the moment, that was all she wanted.

It wasn't until she actually crossed the living room to the dining room that she realized there weren't two men, after all. There were in fact three. It was something she only realized when she felt a hard slap to the side of her face. When she spun around at the blow, the slap was followed by a solid, full-fisted punch to her eye. The baseball bat went crashing to the floor, followed immediately by Annie. Then she was booted hard in the chest, and the air left her lungs in a heavy whoosh.

For a moment, she only lay there, stunned and silent. Then she heard a couple of masculine shouts, a buzzing in her ears, and the rasp of a match striking sandpaper. . . .

Eleven

She'd had no idea fire could spread that quickly. One minute, there was nothing more than a single match burning on the floor a couple of feet in front of her face, and the next, the entire dining room seemed to be ablaze. Annie tried to push herself up on her elbows, but the motion was too much for her and she fell back again, her face smashing against the hardwood floor with a solid thump. Something warm and sticky ran freely from her nose, and she hoped like hell she hadn't broken it.

The buzzing in her ears grew louder and louder, until she finally realized that it wasn't her muddled brain creating the noise, but the smoke detector at the foot of the stairs. She relaxed a little. One thing about the children of Homestead House. They had all been fire-drilled within an inch of their lives.

Moments later, Annie was surrounded by the older kids, all of them brandishing fire extinguishers pointed at the base of the fire. One of the girls—Melody, if Annie remembered correctly—would be across the street at the Gustafsons calling the fire department by now, and Nita would be in the process of herding the smaller children out of the house, if she hadn't done so already. Mickey would—

Mickey.

She didn't realize she'd said his name aloud until Ross, the eldest of Homestead's residents at sixteen, called over his shoulder, "He's okay, Annie. Everybody's outside 'cept us in here. And we're workin' on it. How 'bout you? You okay?"

She nodded weakly, and with a heartfelt groan, pushed herself into a sitting position. She brushed the back of her hand lightly under her nose, and wasn't surprised when it came away smudged with blood. In spite of that, she rose and stumbled into the kitchen, moving awkwardly toward the pantry for the last of the fire extinguishers.

By the time she staggered back, the kids had the fire pretty well under control. When all was said and done, all four dining room walls and a good bit of the floor were black and ravaged, and part of the living room had succumbed briefly to the flames. The braided rug was scorched and smoldering, the walls nearest the dining room smeared with the dusky stains of a water-squelched fire. The pungent aroma of heat and smoke surrounded Annie. In the distance, she heard a siren howl to life.

A trembling overtook her entire body then, shaking her until she thought she could hear her teeth rattle. The extinguisher tumbled from her cold fingers, landing on the floor with a quick *ka-thunk*, and her legs buckled beneath her. And the only thought that wandered through her head was that she had managed to escape death, only to have to face life all alone.

It was an odd reaction, to say the least, and one she fortunately didn't have to consider for very long. What seemed to be an endless onslaught of fire fighters came running through the front door and rushing up the stairs, hustling everyone out of the house. Two of them hauled Annie to her feet, deposited her out on the sidewalk, and demanded to know what had happened.

She recounted what she could while a paramedic checked her over and taped two butterfly bandages over a gash on her cheek. Her nose, the woman assured her as she concluded her checkup, wasn't broken. And her internal organs seemed not to have been affected by the blow to her abdomen. And although she would probably carry that shiner around for a few days, in the long run, the paramedic told her, Annie was going to be just fine.

Annie sputtered a dubious sound at the final segment of the diagnosis and thanked the paramedic, then asked Ross to perform a third head count to make sure everyone was present and accounted for—even though the first two counts had been right on the mark, something he pointed out to her *again*. At her insistence, however, he tallied the group one more time, and this time came up with a count that was off by one.

"No one's missin'," the teenager quickly assured Annie when she jumped to her feet. He smiled and wiggled his eyebrows suggestively. "Just some dude showed up who's askin' about you."

She whipped around to find Ike at the curb, leaning haphazardly against his car with Mickey standing before him, his hands cupped fiercely over the little boy's shoulders. He looked incongruous amid the tumbling red lights of the fire trucks and the general disorder surrounding them, impeccably attired as he was in an elegant tuxedo. Annie arched her brows in surprise, but remained motionless otherwise.

"Are you all right?" he asked, his voice so soft, it scarcely carried from the street to the sidewalk.

She nodded, but said nothing.

He released a slow, steady breath of air, squeezed Mickey's shoulders and released the boy. Mickey turned to gaze up at Ike and smiled. "See? I told ya she'd need ya. She's scared. I can tell."

Annie lifted a hand to her face, felt the butterfly bandages on her cheek and a hard knot forming under her eye. She glanced down at her attire. Her ugly, old blue bathrobe hung open over a ripped Penn State T-shirt and a pair of paisley men's boxer shorts. No telling what her hair looked like.

Then she cursed herself for her wayward thoughts. Someone had just tried to burn down her house, for criminy's sake. Her kids could have been hurt, or even killed. *She* could have been hurt or killed. And she was worried about how she must look to a man who, for all she knew, might have commissioned someone to start the fire to begin with?

Immediately, she knew that wasn't true. In spite of the many, and very confusing, things she felt toward Ike Guthrie, Annie knew without question that he was incapable of pulling something like this. He might be a selfish, thoughtless, greedy pig, but he wasn't the kind of person who would deliberately endanger children. Nevertheless, she felt a bit wary.

"What are you doing here?" she asked him.

"I called him," Mickey interjected before Ike had a chance to explain. "I went with Melody to call the fire guys, and when she was done, I called Ike. He told me to."

Annie's gaze flew to Ike. "You told him to call you in case of fire?" she asked. Maybe he wasn't as innocent in this affair as she thought.

Ike sighed deeply. "I gave him my card a while back and wrote my home phone number and my beeper number on it. I asked him to call me if he ever needed me. Or if..."

"If what?" she encouraged him when he said nothing more.

He ran a big hand restlessly through his hair. "If *you* ever needed me."

"It was a fire, Annie," Mickey stated knowledgeably, as if he knew better than she what had just happened. "You needed someone. You needed Ike."

"What I needed—" she began, but bit off the statement before she could finish it. "What I need is good, stiff—" She halted again. Alcohol was a taboo topic in Homestead House. Too many of the kids were products of alcoholic parents, and a couple of them were recovering themselves. "A good, stiff kick in the pants," she finally concluded. She shoved a hand through her bangs, wincing when her fingers caught and yanked a tangle. "Cripes, what next?" she mumbled.

"I have an idea."

If it was Ike Guthrie's idea, it would be nothing but trouble, she was sure. Still, it was nearly five o'clock in the morning, she was surrounded by a bunch of kids who were way too het up to sleep, she felt like hell herself, and she was fresh out of ideas. For that reason, and that one alone, she replied, "Oh, really? What's that?"

Ike smiled and held up his hand, his fingers extended upward, his thumb folded over his palm. "Four words," he said softly. "International ... House ... of ... Pancakes."

Annie opened her mouth to denounce the idea hotly once and for all, but was shouted down by a chorus of youthful voices who assured her that breakfast was definitely in order.

Ike couldn't remember the last time he'd seen a woman put away seven pancakes. Even he rarely managed more than five. He watched in amazement as Annie sopped up the last of her blueberry syrup with pecan pancake number seven and then reached for number eight. This time she chose maple syrup, pouring it on as generously as she would fill a bathtub with water.

Around them, the children of Homestead House occu-pied an entire corner of the restaurant, laughing and teas-ing each other to release the tension that had lain barely simmering below the surface once the fire had been extin-guished and they'd realized just how badly things could have turned out. Ike, too, would rather think of anything else. Even though he hadn't been a part of the episode, he'd seen the aftermath. It was amazing, really, how little damage had occurred. Even the fire fighters had been surprised. They'd commended the children and Annie for their levelheadedness and excellent planning. And they'd deemed the house safe enough for habitation.

Nevertheless, Ike knew that with the sentiment in the neighborhood being what it was, Annie and her kids were anything but safe at Homestead House. And he figured she knew that, too. Still, he was no closer to an answer or alternative now than he had been weeks ago. And her lawsuit against him and the city helped matters not at all.

"I guess fighting fires makes a person powerful hungry, huh?" he asked quietly as Annie shoved another larger than was actually discreet bite into her mouth.

She smiled guiltily, her cheeks stained with the blush of embarrassment, her chin stained with syrup. "Umm," she mumbled around the mouthful of food. She chewed for a moment, swallowed with some difficulty, and licked the corner of her mouth. "Yeah, I guess it does. Plus, I didn't eat dinner last night."

"Why not?"

"I forgot."

"You forgot to eat dinner."

She nodded and inhaled another bite of pancake, chewing voraciously before swallowing. "I was on the phone all evening. Trying to raise some money." She eyed him critically, her gaze resting on the black silk bow tie that dangled free of his butterfly collar, now opened at the neck. "Looks like you were out spending some."

"I was at the theater," he told her, taking some comfort in what seemed to be a touch of jealousy in her voice.

"Must have been a late show." Her observation was offered dryly, as if she didn't believe that for a minute.

"As a matter of fact, the show was over. I had escorted my date home, and she invited me in for a nightcap." Of course, he decided, there was no reason Annie had to know that his date had been his sister, and that he'd been wheedled into joining Nora for *Madame Butterfly* when her husband had bailed out on her. "We got to talking, and one thing led to another. When Mickey beeped me, I had no idea how late it was."

Annie uttered a derisive sound. "I'll bet. I seem to remember having a couple of conversations like that with you myself."

She blushed again and quickly turned her attention to her breakfast. But it suddenly seemed to hold no appeal for her, because she simply tore at the pancake with her fork and pushed the soggy bits around on her plate. Ike hoped she was worried that he had been making love to another woman as fiercely as he had to her, hoped more that the thought of such a thing enraged Annie to the point of tumbling him to the floor to have her way with him.

Instead she looked up at him again, smiled a dismally false smile and said, "I'm glad you found someone. I wish the two of you well."

Then she winced as she shifted her position on the seat.

Any humor Ike might have been feeling fled with that quietly offered grunt of pain. "They beat you up pretty bad, huh?" he asked. There was barely restrained fury behind his words.

She shook her head. "Actually, it was just one guy who hit me. And only a couple of times at that. He just made them count, is all."

Ike nodded. He looked at the dark red gash on her cheek, the swollen bridge of her nose, the angry purple bruise under her eye. "If I ever find the son of a bitch who did this to you," he said quietly, "I'll kill him."

She eyed him levelly. "Not if I find him first. This is my fight, Ike. Not yours."

"It is my fight, Annie. Anything that concerns you concerns me."

"How do you figure that?"

"Because I love you."

He wasn't sure when he'd decided to reveal that to her. Hell, he wasn't even sure when he'd realized it himself. The words just sort of jumped out of his mouth without warning, but once uttered, he had no way—nor any desire—to take them back. He did love Annie. And oddly enough, it wasn't nearly as difficult to admit that as he had thought it would be. He only hoped he hadn't made a terrible mistake by voicing the sentiment aloud prematurely.

She showed absolutely no reaction to his declaration. She didn't flinch, she didn't smile, she didn't pop him in the mouth. All she did was look at him, blandly and unemotionally, as if she were looking at a piece of carpet lint. Then she picked up her fork and began to push her food around on her plate again.

"I see," she said quietly. "And this woman you were out with last night, she knows that, too?"

"Yes, she does," Ike told her honestly. Hell, just about the only thing he'd talked to Nora about last night had been Annie. It had been scary, to say the least, when, right in the middle of him discussing his fears for her safety, he had been summoned by Mickey, who had confirmed them for him.

"Well, my, my, my," she said mildly. "What an understanding lover you have. How convenient. Of course, you do always look for someone who's convenient when you size up a lover, don't you, Ike? God knows I was."

The accusation stung, but he couldn't quite convince himself that he hadn't deserved it. "I wasn't with a lover last night, Annie. The woman I went to the theater with was my sister. And trust me, she's always been anything but convenient," he added with a halfhearted chuckle. When she didn't respond or look up at him, he added, "And you were never convenient, either."

"Wasn't I?"

He shook his head silently, certainly.

"Sure felt like it."

When she pushed herself out of the booth, Ike could tell she was trying to make a fast break. Unfortunately, her stiff, pain-racked body made that impossible. It was obviously uncomfortable for her, but it worked well to his advantage. He was in the aisle before she was, standing in front of her to block her way to her kids.

"You're not going to say anything?" he asked her. "I tell you that I love you, and you don't even have the decency to offer me a response?"

She looked up at him, her expression bland. "Oh, you mean you were *serious* about that?"

"Of course I was serious. How can you even ask that?"

She pushed past him, then turned and walked backward toward the children. As she went, she said, "Look, Ike, I have a full day ahead of me. A burned-out couple of rooms I need to clean up, a house to ventilate, kids to take care of, homicidal neighbors with arsonous tendencies to confront, money to beg for in order to survive...." She paused, stopping before she got within earshot of her brood.

"I've got kids to keep safe," she told him softly. "I've got to do whatever's necessary to preserve something I believe in—something that's right and good and decent. I don't sell out to the highest bidder like a whore, I won't settle for lesser alternatives that might be temporarily convenient in order to bring the profit margin up, and I will not surrender my children's welfare without fighting to my last breath. So you'll understand when I tell you I really don't have time to stand here and swap jokes with you, right?"

She turned her back again, but Ike followed and clapped a hand over her shoulder, then spun her around to face him. "You think that's what I do?" he asked softly. "You think I'm a whore? That the only thing that's important to me is money? That I'd rather give up on you and the kids than give up on this project?"

She eyed him thoughtfully for a moment. "Okay then, you tell me. What's the most important thing in the world to you, Ike? The *most important thing*. Be honest."

There was a time not so long ago when he would have been able to answer her question immediately. Respect and power and prestige. And, yes, money, too. Those were the most important things. He wanted wealth. He wanted his name in the paper. He wanted to be somebody, and that's what he'd thought it took. Since meeting Annie Malone, however, his ideas about importance, his sense of right and wrong, of good and bad, had shifted some.

Still, he couldn't answer her right away. Because he realized, much to his horror, that at the moment, he didn't know for sure what was the most important thing in the world to him.

Annie, he told himself. Surely, Annie must be the most important thing. But if that was true, why hadn't he been fighting harder for her? Why had he simply backed off the moment things between them had become complicated?

"Yeah, that's what I thought," she said, snapping him out of his troubled musing. Her voice softened as she added, "Look, don't get me wrong, Ike. I said before that you're a good guy, and I still believe that deep down inside, you are. But I don't think you've ever really taken the time to think about where you're going, where you've been. You're good at the short-term stuff. And I think you sometimes believe the things you tell yourself. But the real world is nothing like the world you've created for yourself to live in. And if you ask me, it must be suffocating to have to live in yours the way you do."

With that left hanging between them, Annie went to gather her brood. They'd come to the restaurant in taxis, for which Ike had naturally paid, and they made it clear with vociferous acknowledgement that they wanted to go home the same way. But Annie herded them outside to a bus stop without consulting Ike about return fare, without even saying goodbye.

He was accustomed to being in control of a situation, and in control of the people surrounding him. Yet Annie Malone was one confounding situation, and she was clearly a human being that defied control. Somehow, Ike had managed to fall in love with an ungovernable power. One that had him questioning just about everything he'd ever considered to be right and true. And he had no idea what to do about it.

Dammit, that woman was going to drive him insane yet.

It was no use. It was over. There was nothing she could do now. Annie scanned the letter in her hand for the fourth time, then sat down hard on the sofa. The courts had spoken. And they had found favor with the city, upholding its contract with Buchanan-Guthrie Designs, Inc. Motion denied, score one for the defense, but, hey, thanks for playing. Annie dropped her head into her hands. Not even a lousy garment bag for a door prize.

And as if it weren't enough that she'd lost her case, the letter went on to inform her that the point was moot, anyway, because Homestead House was no longer viable, no longer necessary, no longer welcome. But if she wanted to move it outside the city limits...

Annie lifted her head to stare out at the living room, but she saw nothing but a haze of red before her eyes. They were going to take her house from her. They were going to take her kids. They were going to take her life.

The one thing she had worked so hard to maintain for nearly a decade, the one thing she'd put her entire life's work into, the one thing that had been more important to her than anything else in the world... gone. Just like that. By the end of the summer, the letter told her, every resident of Homestead House was to be well and truly vacated from the premises. Her children were to be placed in city-run foster care, and she was essentially out of a job.

It didn't bother her much to be unemployed. Hell, truth be told, it didn't even bother her that much to be losing Homestead House. In spite of Ike's efforts to improve the place, it was still an eyesore, and the neighborhood was dangerous. *Hate* was a word Annie normally prohibited from use in her home. But she hated, she *hated* losing her kids.

And she hated having to be the one to tell them the news. Hated being the one who was going to have to make the arrangements that would separate them and send them to live with strangers who couldn't possibly love them as much as she did or care for them as well. She hated it that she would be denied the opportunity to watch them grow into healthy, happy adults and share in their achievements and successes.

She wished she could hate Ike Guthrie, too.

Unfortunately, ever since seeing the devastated look on his face that morning she'd asked him what was most important to him in the world, she'd been overcome by something else entirely. She wasn't sure exactly what she'd seen there—uncertainty, perhaps, or even regret. He had looked like a man who was facing his conscience for the first time in his entire life and not much liking what he saw. He had looked hurt. Confused. Nothing at all like the Ike Guthrie she had become accustomed to seeing.

He had told her he loved her that morning three weeks ago. And she'd wished with all her heart that she could believe him. Because in spite of everything that had occurred, she still cared about Ike. She no longer blamed him for what had happened to Homestead House. She could even believe him now when he told her he hadn't realized initially how his company's stake in the renovation was going to turn her life completely upside down. She'd been hurt and angry at the prospect of losing her kids, and he'd been a convenient target for venting her hostility and frustration.

But no man could have made love to her as he did without caring about what happened to her, she thought. No man. It was something she was only now beginning to realize.

Nevertheless, he wasn't the man she had let herself believe him to be, or that she had hoped he would become.

Before, she had been so impressed by his confidence and foresight, that she hadn't let herself acknowledge the potential for damage such characteristics could wreak. Ike Guthrie, she realized now, was little more than a cliché—he was one of those guys who just didn't have their priorities straight. And he would probably never understand exactly how deeply that would affect his life.

She still considered him to be a good guy. She just hadn't realized how deeply buried the goodness in him was. If it hadn't surfaced by now, she thought, then it was going to take someone with better mining skills than she possessed to bring that goodness, that decency, to light. She'd been close, and maybe if she had more time, she might be able to tap it. But right now, she had more pressing matters to see to.

Annie leaned back against the sofa, tipping her head back to stare at the ceiling. But as hard as she tried to banish thoughts of Ike, the man's face kept circling before her mind's eye, his expression wavering between the one he'd worn when he'd told her he loved her and the one he'd displayed when she'd asked him what was most important to him in the world. From utter confidence to utter confusion. Annie squeezed her eyes shut and, with much effort, she pushed the image away and thought instead of her kids.

Her kids. Oh, boy, how was she going to tell her kids?

The house was an eyesore. The paint—what was left of it—was a horrific shade of orange that had blistered and faded under the sun. The windows were cracked and filthy, the shutters were gone. The roof was growing things no garden would ever support. The stairs were sagging and old and would have to be replaced. The yard didn't appear to have been tended to since the Eisenhower administration. The kitchen smelled like a cat box. But the place was cheap. And it was up to code. In other words, it was perfect.

Ike made one more quick pass through the house, then circled the grounds in his Jeep. Oh, yeah, he thought. This place was perfect.

Annie was going to love it.

Twelve

Twelve

"This is it? This is the place?"

Annie shielded her eyes against the early morning sun that hung low over the house in question. She didn't sound nearly as enthusiastic as Ike had hoped she would. In fact, she sounded as if she wanted to kill him.

"This is the place," he told her, trying to inject a little more optimism into his voice than he currently felt. "Isn't it great? Don't you love it? Won't it be perfect for you and the kids?"

She turned to stare at him, mouth gaping, eyebrows arrowed down in disbelief. "You have *got* to be kidding. You think I'm going to turn my kids loose in a house that's going to go tumbling down around their ears two minutes after they enter it? I'd rather see them take their chances with foster care."

Ike shook his head vehemently and jumped down from the Jeep. "No, no, no, that's not true at all." He strode easily, confidently toward the front porch and settled a foot on the bottom step, then stomped hard to illustrate just how hardy the place was. Unfortunately, his foot went right through the wood and splashed into a mud puddle beneath.

"Um, okay, so the steps have a little problem with rot," he conceded as he shook the water from his damp hiking boot. "The foundation of the building itself really *is* solid. In fact, even though it might not look like it, the whole structure is perfectly sound. I checked it out myself."

Annie sat back down in the Jeep and nodded indulgently, clearly indicating it was time for them to leave. "Um, yeah, okay. Listen, Ike, it was nice of you to try to help out and everything, but—"

"And I've verified that with the county and the bank, too," he interrupted her before she could voice her protest. "Yes, they want to unload this place badly, but they'd never do it if they thought someone would get hurt. If nothing else, they're terrified of being sued." He smiled at her. "Your reputation has preceded you, even here in beautiful Bucks County. Instilling that fear of lawsuit alone, I got them to knock another five grand off the price."

Annie stood again, looking lovely and indignant in her faded jeans and even more faded sleeveless blue work shirt. She jumped down from the Jeep and crossed the yard, scattering crickets and grasshoppers from the knee-high grass in her wake. When she halted in front of him, she frowned at him. "Ike, what the hell is going on?"

His smile fell. "What do you mean?"

"I mean in less than a week, the movers are coming to take my stuff and put it in storage, and the state's coming to take my kids and put them in public facilities. And you show up at my door totally out of the blue and tell me I *have* to come with you, that there's this place I absolutely *must* see, and that I'll never forgive myself if I pass up this *incredible* opportunity."

"Yeah, so what's your point?"

She threw her arms open wide, indicating the house. "So *this* is the must-see, incredible opportunity?"

He rocked back proudly on his heels, his smile returning full force. "Yup. You can thank me later."

"I'd rather strangle you now."

He held his hands up, palms out, in a gesture of surrender. "Look, Annie, just bear with me for a minute. Open your mind. Look beyond the limitations you see in front of you. Forget about everything that's come before today."

He hoped he was making it clear to her that he was talking about more than the house. A lot more. "Just give me one chance to show you how much potential is here, okay?"

She folded her arms over her midsection and sighed. Finally, she acceded, "Okay. Show me what you've got."

He wished he could take her statement more personally, more explicitly, but the look in her eyes told him she was feeling anything but sexually frisky right now. Ike sighed. He had his work cut out for him if he ever hoped to convince her that he'd finally figured out what was the most important thing in the world.

After he'd parted ways with Annie that morning a few weeks ago, he'd returned to his office and asked himself the question she had posed. And he'd thought hard about it, too, about what was most important to him in the world. And surprisingly, he'd only had to think about it for a little while. Then he'd picked up the phone and started making a few calls. In no time at all, he'd become the most focused man alive.

"This used to be a farm until about three years ago," he began, helping her up over the first step, taking care not to snap any more in two. Her hand in his felt good, and he realized it had been more than a month since he'd had any physical contact with her. How odd that he had managed to make it through a day, let alone a month, without it.

"So what happened three years ago?" she asked him.

"That's when the couple who owned the property were killed in an accident. Because they'd mortgaged the place to the nines, the bank came into ownership. They've been trying to sell it ever since, but as you can see, the house needs a lot of work, and the grounds have been untended for a long time, and it's going to take an army to fix it up."

She expelled an errant breath of air that blew her hair off her forehead. "You got that right."

Ike waited until she looked at him again, and then he grinned at her. "Or else a houseful of kids and one very determined social worker hoping to give them a sense of purpose in their lives."

Annie opened her mouth to say something, then snapped it shut again. She looked out over the yard and surveyed the sagging barn and silo in the distance. She turned to consider the house behind her. As she did so, Ike could almost see the wheels turning in her brain.

"The best part about it," he went on, knowing one could never lay it on too thick when trying to win someone else's approval, "is that because there's about three acres of land that isn't used for farming, it would be a piece of cake to build a couple more structures to house more kids—and more social workers. And even though you'd probably never get the farm back up and running the way it was back when it was most prosperous, you could earn some decent money with the apple orchard. And that barn over there is a dairy facility. And there's a pond you could stock with fish."

The look on her face told him she was seriously considering his vision of the future. So Ike laid it on even thicker. "Really," he continued in a matter-of-fact tone, "when you get right down to it, the possibilities for making a fair income with this place are endless. Never mind the wide open spaces, clean sky, fresh air and obvious absence of street crime, gangs and gunfire. Oh, yeah. And your nearest neighbors are miles away, so no one's going to be muttering, 'There goes the neighborhood' when you and the kids take possession."

When Annie turned to smile at him, he was surprised to discover that her eyes reflected sadness instead of hope or triumph. "It's a nice dream, Ike," she said quietly. "And I appreciate your sharing it with me. But that's all it is. A dream."

"It's only a dream for now," he told her. "It could very easily become a reality."

"Sure, with thousands and thousands of dollars I don't have."

He wiggled his eyebrows playfully. "Not a problem."

"Very big problem," she assured him otherwise.

He shook his head, but said only, "Take a walk with me. There's a beautiful spot up over that hill I want you to see."

She joined him, listening patiently as he went on more about what a great find this property was, and how it wouldn't take long to turn it into a facility for kids that included horses, arts and crafts and camping. He waxed poetic about how many more lives Annie and others like her could save and guide, how many kids would benefit, and how greatly at that, because she had so much more room and so little danger of the urban sprawl creeping in. She wouldn't have to beg for money the way she used to, he pointed out, because the place could potentially generate enough to keep itself up and running.

They could call it The Homestead.

He described opportunities. Envisioned an entire way of life. And although Annie smiled and nodded, he knew she didn't believe him for a minute.

"This is the place," he said when they topped a small green hill that overlooked a sparkling pond and nothing but more green hills in the distance.

He led her down to the bank of the pond, where the tall grass receded to springy clover, and then to a dusty embankment.

"You're right," she said. "It's beautiful here."

"It's a nice place to sit and think. Or chat. Or whatever."

She eyed him suspiciously, but he forced himself to remain on his best behavior. "Take your shoes off."

Her eyebrows shot up in surprise. "What?"

"Take your shoes off. You won't believe how warm the water in this pond is. And there are a million frogs. You'll love it."

He dropped to sit on the ground and began to unlace his hiking boots. With an idle sigh, Annie joined him, her boots and socks joining his as she wiggled her bare toes in the clover. Ike lay down and folded a forearm beneath his head and watched the white clouds above him slip slowly by. Annie, he noted, remained seated beside him, crossing her legs Indian-fashion, leaning back on her hands, turning her face to the warmth of the sun.

"You once told me," he said quietly, "that the reason you didn't like me was because I had a position in the community I didn't use to its full potential. Do you remember that?"

She chuckled as she turned to look at him. "Yeah. Back in Cape May. Another lifetime ago."

"Well, at the time, I wasn't convinced you were right. I figured nobody was going to donate money to a cause just because someone else did a little arm-twisting."

"They don't necessarily," she told him. "It depends on who's holding their arm and how much muscle that person has to flex." She held up her own arm, hardening her biceps. "As you can see, I don't have that much. In spite of years of flexing them as powerfully as I can."

Ike, too, held up his arm, pushing back the sleeve of his smoky gray T-shirt to reveal a muscle that was big, solid and very well defined. "Me, on the other hand...somehow I wound up with quite a bit without ever trying to flex them. Even so, I didn't realize quite how much until I started making phone calls."

Annie dropped her hand back to the ground, then, after a moment, stretched out on her side in the clover beside Ike. "What kind of phone calls?"

"Some that might help out you and the kids. At first, it surprised me to discover a lot of my friends and colleagues weren't interested in contributing money to a facility that would enable troubled kids to turn their lives around."

She skimmed a hand lightly over the fragrant clover and sighed. "I don't like to say I told you so, but—"

"But it surprised me even more how quickly they changed their minds when I started reminding them of the favors they owed me, or how I'd done this or that thing for them years ago, or how if they didn't put up some cold hard cash, I'd never do business with them again, or about how I knew they did this thing or that thing that wasn't exactly ethical, never mind *legal*, and—"

Her hand stilled in the clover, and she glanced up at him from beneath lowered lids. "Ike, you didn't."

He closed his eyes and inhaled deeply of the sunny morning, and pretended not to hear her. "All of a sudden, the pledges started rolling in. I could hear their checkbooks flip open even as we spoke. It was amazing. I had no idea I held such a prominent position in the community."

Annie bit her lip and stared at the man lying so casually beside her, his eyes closed to the glare of the sun, the wind ruffling his hair as if nudging a butterfly's wings. She smiled. "Ike?"

"Yes?"

"What have you done?"

He inhaled another deep breath, released it slowly, then opened one eye. "I've got a whole bunch of money to give you, Annie. And all kinds of sponsors have pledged their troth to you and your brood. Everything from lumber corporations to independent fruit stand operators are all nicely placed to help you out in whatever way they can."

She smiled. "You didn't."

He smiled back. "I did."

"You did?"

He opened his other eye and nodded. "Mmm-hmm."

"Why?"

He, too, rolled to his side, and caught a fistful of her hair in his hand. "I think I already told you that once, and you didn't believe me."

"So tell me again."

He moved his hand to cup her cheek. "Because I love you, Annie. I love you."

"You do?"

"I do."

Instead of replying, she leaned forward and kissed him, a brief brush of her lips over his. "Well, why didn't you say so?" she asked quietly when she pulled away.

This time it was Ike who kissed her in response. He curved his hand around her nape and urged her head down toward his, touching his mouth tenderly to hers. "I thought I did," he whispered against her lips.

She shook her head slowly. "No, that wasn't you who told me you loved me. That was some guy who had his priorities all mixed up. You're different from him."

He tipped his head forward until his forehead pressed gently against hers. "In what way?"

She hesitated for only a moment. "Unlike that other guy, you know what's really important. You know what the most important thing in the world is."

"Is that the only way I differ?"

She shook her head. "No. I didn't love that guy."

"But you love this one?"

She nodded.

"Then why don't you say so?"

She pulled back only enough to gaze levelly into his eyes. What she saw there nearly knocked the breath right out of her, and she knew at once that everything he was telling her was true. She placed her palm gently over his rough cheek and threaded her fingers through his hair. "I love you, Ike. I love you."

"Well, it's about time we got that settled."

Laughing, he pulled her down to him and rolled until she lay beneath him. He tangled his legs with hers, and propped himself up on elbows and forearms planted firmly on the ground on each side of her head. Effectively penned, Annie saw no alternative but to wrap her arms around his waist and hold him close.

His near-white hair tumbled down over his forehead, his clear blue eyes shone with more love and contentment than she'd ever seen another human being display. His warm breath caressed her neck and chest where her shirt collar was open. He smelled much like the sunny morning and the sweet clover surrounding them. And he was hers. All hers. Maybe her sister had paid for him, but Ike was Annie's man.

"Kiss me."

She wasn't sure who spoke the words, just that they seemed to hang in the air between them for several moments before either of them obeyed. And then Ike was lowering his head to hers, nibbling her lips, tasting the corners of her mouth, slipping his tongue between her teeth to carry her further away.

After that, things grew a little hazy for Annie. She felt his fingers on the buttons of her shirt, unfastening each from its mooring until he pushed the softly worn chambray away to expose the white undershirt beneath. His palm closed over one breast, rubbing the cotton covering it until the friction of the two together agitated the peak to ripening. She felt him swell against her thigh, and shifted to accommodate him more fully. With an almost imperceptible sigh, he cradled himself between her legs, pressing his burgeoning staff more intimately against her, until Annie, too, sighed with delight.

She tugged his shirt from the waistband of his jeans, shoving her hands beneath to rove at will over the warm skin of his back. She gloried in every dip and swell of solid muscle she encountered, fingered his ribs one by one. Then her hands seemed to travel of their own accord to furrow between their bodies, fairly ripping his shirt completely from his jeans so that she could explore the man more thoroughly.

Before she realized his intent, Ike broke free of her embrace long enough to reach behind himself, to jerk the shirt over his head and toss it to the ground near their boots. He towered over her, straddling her, his naked torso hers to explore at her leisure. But leisurely was the last thing she felt. She lifted her hands to his chest, scraping her fingers through the soft, springy blond hair scattered abundantly across it, then, with one fingertip, traced the downy line to his navel and beyond.

Ike sucked in a deep breath, his belly becoming concave when he did so, and Annie dipped her fingers into the waistband of his jeans to flick open the first button. Then the second. Then the third...

Ike caught her wrist with firm fingers and cautioned, "You might want to hold off on those last two."

Annie arched her brows, hoping to appear innocent, when in fact she felt as brazen as the very devil himself. "Oh? Why's that?"

Instead of replying with words, he grinned, a feral, not-quite-satisfied expression darkening his face. He bent forward again and kissed her, then removed his leg from between hers and lay down alongside her. Annie rolled to her side to face him, and he ran an idle finger down her bare arm. She shivered in spite of the sun's glaring heat.

"Come closer," he said softly.

She scooted nearer.

"Closer," he encouraged her.

She scooted nearer still.

"Closer," he instructed her further.

She moved until her body was flush with his and smiled. "What's the old Marx Brothers bit? If I were any closer to you I'd be behind you?"

Ike chuckled low. "We'll get to that eventually."

"Ike..."

He twined her fingers with his and brought them to his lips, kissing each one and her palm before settling her hand over his heart. "There you go again. Saying my name as if you were uttering an incantation."

She shook her head. "Not an incantation. A benediction. For you are, without question, the answer to every prayer I've ever sent skyward."

He closed his eyes, as if he didn't know quite how to respond to her statement. When he opened them again, they seemed clearer and bluer than before somehow. Annie knew it was impossible for eyes to change in such a way, but there was a peaceful quality there that she hadn't noticed before. A certainty, perhaps, or maybe a serenity.

"I don't want to lose you," he said. "Ever."

"You won't have to," she vowed.

"Do you promise?"

"Yes."

"Will you make it legal?"

She bit her lip. "That depends."

"On what?"

She hesitated only a moment before saying with a chuckle, "On whether you intend to marry me or adopt me."

Ike laughed a little, sounding relieved. "I want to marry *you*," he said softly. "It's...it's Mickey I'd like to adopt. I mean...if you think...that is, if he's amenable to the arrangement, too."

Annie smiled. "Gee, what a coincidence. I was kind of hoping to adopt Mickey myself someday. But the officials always told me it would be difficult to do, seeing as how I would be a single parent. Maybe together, the two of us can manage to win what we couldn't alone." She kissed his cheek softly. "And, don't worry. I think Mickey will be delighted to have a father like you."

"A father," Ike repeated. "Now that's a label I never thought I'd be attaching to myself." After a moment, another thought seemed to hit him. "Good God. I'm going to be the father of your entire brood, aren't I?"

She smiled. "Yeah, I'd say the chances of that are pretty good."

He shook his head slowly, seeming to just now understand exactly what he'd gotten himself into with Annie. "Boy, there's going to be an awful lot that needs doing around here. I'm going to have to cut back at work."

She nodded. "That's probably not a bad idea."

"Maybe Chase and I can take on another partner. That would free up more of my time for...oh, building more stuff around here, helping you manage the place—"

"Having more kids."

"Oh, sure we'll have more kids around here. There should be plenty of room. Maybe you can get together with a couple of state agencies to—"

"No," she interrupted him gently, "I mean having more kids."

Ike gazed at her, obviously confused.

"You know," she said helpfully, "*having more kids*. As in the two of us having more kids. Together. You and me."

"You and me?" he repeated.

She nodded. "You and me." When he said nothing more, she asked, "Don't you want to have kids?"

"I...I never really thought about it. Do you?"

"Well...yeah."

He said nothing more for a moment, then seemed to realize he was simply lying there, staring at her. He blinked, as if that would break the spell, and said, "Okay. When can we do it?"

Annie glanced down at their entwined, half-clothed bodies, then back at Ike. "I thought we were doing it now."

His gaze followed hers, as if he'd forgotten for a moment what had commanded their attention only moments ago. He pushed the strap of her undershirt off her shoulder and bent to kiss the top of her breast. "So we are," he said softly when he lifted his head again. "Then we can do the marriage and adoption thing later. And the kid thing, too. Although," he added as an afterthought, "I didn't exactly come prepared for this. The kid thing could happen sooner than later."

Annie nodded and reached for the fourth button of his blue jeans. "Okay."

"Okay?" he echoed. "Just like that?"

She plucked open the fifth and final button and tucked her hand inside the open fly. Ike swelled to life against her palm. She grinned. "Just like that."

After that, words became unnecessary. Annie sat up long enough to shed her undershirt, and before the garment hit the ground, Ike had gathered her close again. He buried his face in the curve of her neck and shoulder, dragging an openmouthed kiss from her earlobe to her shoulder to the pink, velvety tip of her breast. He curved his palm over her jeans-clad derriere and pulled her into his lap, facing himself. Then he covered her breast more completely with his mouth.

Annie hooked her ankles together at the base of his spine and tangled her fingers in his hair, clutching his head to her bosom. His hands raced open-palm over her naked back, cupping her shoulder blades as tenderly as he had her breasts, tracing the column of her spine with his thumb, dipping his fingers into her jeans to sneak below the fabric of her panties. He pushed cotton and denim down to bare her bottom, palming the warm flesh firmly as he lifted her higher toward his hungry mouth. Annie's ankles unlatched, and she rose to her knees before him, too weak to do anything else but enjoy the ministrations of his lips and tongue.

And then she felt herself falling slowly backward, felt the cool crush of clover beneath her bare back and thighs, and knew that Ike had at some point completed her undressing. When he stretched out atop her, anchoring himself on his forearms, fists clenching her hair, he, too, was naked. His damp skin seemed to fuse with hers everywhere he touched her. She hitched her calves over his to moor him in place, clenched his taut buttocks in her hands and urged him closer still.

When she lifted her head to kiss his neck, his throat, his jaw, she tasted salt, sweat and sunshine. He turned his head to lock his mouth with hers, fairly sucking the life from her when he drew her tongue into his mouth. For a moment, Annie forgot where she was, who she was, what her needs in life should be. Then she remembered. She was here, she was a woman, she needed him. At that moment, nothing else mattered but the warm summer morning, and two people who had discovered love and hope reveling in their newfound emotions.

Ike lowered himself to his elbows and caught her breasts in both hands. He kissed and suckled the rigid peak of one, then the other, then skimmed his lips lower down her body, pausing at the juncture of her thighs. He loved her as he had that night that seemed a lifetime ago. And when he traced a line back up along her damp torso with his tongue, she wrestled him over onto his back and loved him in exactly the same way.

He shuddered as she circled him one final time with her tongue and then raked the pad of her thumb over the tip of his shaft. She moved to sit astride him, but before she completed the action, he swept her off and clamored atop her, burying himself so deeply inside her, he was certain she would snap in two. But instead of breaking, Annie arched her hips to greet him, seizing the backs of his thighs to drive him further inside her still.

There was no way he could control himself after that. He bucked and writhed against her, scoring her so thoroughly, their bodies were dragged over the ground. Over and over again, Ike pelted her, and over and over again, Annie opened to accommodate him in his entirety. Finally, the shudder of completion rocked him, and he felt her quake and contract around him. At the same time he slumped over her, her body went limp beneath him. Nei-

ther of them seemed able to do more than breathe deeply,
trying to regain enough oxygen to bring sense back to their
brains, and strength back to their bodies.

Ike was the first to move. But he didn't go far. He lifted
himself off Annie only enough to notice that they were a
good five feet further from their clothing than they had
been when they started their exploration. "Wow," he
murmured when he looked at her face again. "The earth
really did move. That's never happened to me before."

She raised her head to note their new position, then lowered it back to the ground with a chuckle. "I don't even
want to think about explaining the grass stains on my
tushie."

He arched an eyebrow curiously. "Is anyone else going
to be seeing your tushie any time in the near future?"

She shook her head.

"Then no explanation will be necessary, will it?"

"I guess not. But who wants a green tushie on her wedding night?"

Ike smiled and managed to draw enough strength from
somewhere to roll them both to their sides. "I don't know.
Sounds kind of kinky to me. Could be fun."

Annie started to offer him some smart remark, then
gazed over his shoulder and frowned. "Uh-oh. Could be
poison ivy."

Ike did jump up at that. "*What?*"

Annie laughed and pointed to their left. "Over there. But
don't worry. I don't think we rolled in any of it." She eyed
the clump of red-green leaves again and idly scratched her
thigh. "I don't think."

Ike, too, seemed to suddenly feel itchy. He dragged his
fingernails over his elbow. "First thing we do, we'll get rid
of all that."

Suddenly realizing they were sitting in the middle of nowhere completely naked, Annie reached for her clothes.
While she dressed, she seemed to be considering everything that lay ahead of them. "I think before we get around

to yard work, we need to get the house in shape. After all," she added with a smile as she buttoned up her shirt, "the movers are coming in less than a week."

Ike watched her as she dressed, hoping he didn't look as wistful as he felt, then reluctantly reached for his own clothes. "I guess we're going to need all the help we can get. But between your kids and my newly discovered talent for extortion, we should be able to get the house pretty well cleaned up by then. We can work on the cosmetic improvements after everyone's in."

Annie tucked her shirt into her jeans and buttoned them up, then strode barefoot to the banks of the pond. Ike let her go, watching as she gazed out silently over the shimmering surface of the water, sensing that she needed to be alone for a moment. But after a moment, when he couldn't tolerate even that small separation from her, he joined her, looping an arm around her waist, pulling her close.

"What are you thinking about?" he asked her.

She expelled a restless breath. "Just that . . ." She sighed again heavily and leaned back against him. "I've been working so hard for so many years to keep Homestead House alive. I've spent so much time focusing on the present, on the day-to-day survival of the place, that I never stopped to think about the future. Even when Mark was alive, we never made plans for anything. Never."

She turned to face Ike, joining her hands behind his back, gazing up into his eyes. "With you, I'm making plans. I'm seeing a future. And I don't feel like I'm going to have to get up every morning and *fight* someone or something just to get through the day. With you...now..." She smiled. "I feel like I can rest for a little while."

He smiled back. "If you ever have to fight someone again, Annie, I'll be right there by your side. And if you ever need to rest, I'll take up the slack while you sleep. You're not in this alone anymore." He pulled her against him and rested his chin on the top of her head. Quietly, so

quietly he wasn't sure she'd even be able to hear him, he
added, "And neither am I."

She squeezed him gently then, and he knew she had
heard him. Neither said much of anything after that. They
simply stood holding each other, staring out over the green
hills and glittering pond, knowing they'd never have to be
alone again, admitting for the first time just how terrified
of such a prospect they'd always been. Annie tightened her
hold on Ike, and Ike turned to settle his cheek against the
crown of her head.

"I love you," she said softly.

"I love you, too."

And that, they each knew, was the most important thing
in the world.

Epilogue

"You know, when I bought him for you, I knew the two of you would ultimately wind up together." Sophie looked over at Annie and frowned. "But I meant that *you* should become a part of *his* life-style, not that you should drag him down into yours. Annie, you've ruined a perfectly good man."

Annie smiled and gazed fondly at the white gold band that circled the fourth finger of her left hand. "That's not what he thinks," she told her sister softly. "Now shut up and have a piece of cake."

She was spared Sophie's reply when the two of them were surrounded by a laughing, riotous group of children who hugged and kissed her and offered again their congratulations. The girls cooed over Annie's champagne-colored wedding dress, a simple, sleeveless sheath whose scooped neckline was dotted with tiny silk flowers. A chaplet of baby's breath crowned her head, and her hair was twined into a loose braid, gathered at the end with a silk ribbon. When he had first glimpsed her in her wedding finery, Ike had told her she looked like a sienna reprint from *Life* magazine, circa 1969. Then he had smiled and kissed the end of her nose and made her promise never to change.

Now they were surrounded by friends and family in the expansive front yard of their new house, The Homestead. The pale orange monstrosity had been transformed as if by magic into a whitewashed farmhouse whose perimeter boasted flower beds and vegetable gardens, whose lawn was lush and green and well tended. The occupants of the original Homestead House had taken up residence with Annie a month ago, and with pride and purpose had turned the property around.

Ike had designed two new outbuildings, one to house more kids, one to accommodate more social workers, and a work crew was coming next week to begin construction on those and reconstruction on the dairy barn and silo. The orchards had been cleared and readied for autumn, and Annie lifted her nose to the sweet aroma of apples. Ike's dream for the place—the dream he had then shared with her—was fast becoming a reality. Alone, she had always been forced to struggle and fight to keep even a leaky roof over her kids' heads. With Ike, the two of them would be giving the children so much more.

She glanced over at her husband then, who stood with his sister and brother-in-law in the shade of a sweeping maple tree. He smiled at her and lifted his glass in a silent toast, and Annie felt her cheeks grow warm. The pale blue September sky was stained with the pinks and oranges of the dying sunlight, and a warm breeze whispered through the leaves overhead. She was surrounded by her kids, her loved ones, her family. And she would never have to fear losing any of them again. The day was almost perfect.

Almost. Only one thing was missing that would make it consummate.

Annie crossed the yard to take Ike's hand in hers, and she led him back to the banks of the pond where they'd been joined in matrimony less than an hour ago, joined even more intimately some weeks before that. She circled his waist with her arms and hooked her fingers loosely at his back. She had so much to tell him, but for a long time, she said nothing. And when Ike seemed unable to tolerate her silence, he pulled her close and sighed into her hair.

"Nice wedding, huh?" he asked softly.

She nodded against his shoulder.

"Nice house, too."

She nodded again. "And plenty of room," she finally said.

This time Ike was the one to nod. "Yeah, no problems there. Kids on the second and third floor, and you and me with the first all to ourselves."

"Well, maybe not *all* to ourselves," she said, glancing up at him tentatively as she uttered the words.

Ike looked down to meet her gaze. He smiled, and she realized he knew exactly what she had meant by what she had thought a cryptic comment. Nevertheless, his only response was, "Oh?"

She tried to wet her lips, but her mouth seemed to have gone dry. "Actually, we, um, we do still have about eight months of solitude, but after that . . ."

His smile grew broader, lighting his eyes with laughter. "After that . . . ?"

She snuggled closer against him. "After that . . . after that we're going to have another life to touch."

She heard a chuckle erupt deep inside him, then it warmed the air above her head like a breath of summer. "My God, I really am the father of a brood, aren't I?"

"Yup." She tipped her head back to smile at him. "But you knew the job was dangerous when you took it."

He curved his palm over her nape and lowered his head to hers. "That I did," he said just before he kissed her. "But as hazards go," he added when he lifted his face from hers again, "I don't mind taking my chances with you and your kids."

"Our kids," Annie corrected him.

"Our kids," he agreed with a smile.

Ike kissed his wife again, losing himself in her softness, her fragrance, her warmth, thinking this family stuff was something he should have tried years ago.

*   *   *   *   *

SILHOUETTE® *Desire*

COMING NEXT MONTH

#1009 THE COWBOY AND THE KID—Anne McAllister

July's *Man of the Month*, rodeo cowboy Taggart Jones, vowed never to remarry, but his little girl had other plans for him—and every one involved feisty schoolmarm Felicity Albright.

#1010 A GIFT FOR BABY—Raye Morgan

The Baby Shower

All Hailey Kingston wanted was to go to her friend's baby shower. Instead, she was stuck on a remote ranch, with a handsome cowboy as her keeper. But the longer she stayed in Mitch Harper's arms, the less she wanted to leave!

#1011 THE BABY NOTION—Dixie Browning

Daddy Knows Last

Priscilla Barrington wanted a baby, so she planned a visit to the town sperm bank. But then she met Jake Spencer! Could she convince the rugged cowboy to father her child—the old-fashioned way?

#1012 THE BRIDE WORE BLUE—Cindy Gerard

Northern Lights Brides

When Maggie Adams returned home, she never expected to see her childhood neighbor Blue Hazzard. Could the former gawky teenager turned hunk teach Maggie how to love again?

#1013 GAVIN'S CHILD—Caroline Cross

Bachelors and Babies

Gavin Cantrell was stunned to return home and learn that his estranged wife Annie had given birth to his child without telling him. Now that he was back, would his dream of being a family man be fulfilled?

#1014 MONTANA FEVER—Jackie Merritt

Made in Montana

Independent Lola Fanon never met anyone as infuriating—or as irresistible—as Duke Sheridan. She knew he wasn't her type, but staying away from the handsome rancher was becoming a losing battle....

Take 4 bestselling love stories FREE

Plus get a FREE surprise gift!

SILHOUETTE® Desire®
CELEBRATION 1000

A treasured piece of romance could be yours!

During April, May and June as part of Desire's Celebration 1000 you can enter to win an original piece of art used on an actual Desire cover!

Or you could win one of 300 autographed Man of the Month books!

See Official Sweepstakes Rules for more details.

To enter, complete an Official Entry Form or a 3"x5" card by hand printing "Silhouette Desire Celebration 1000 Sweepstakes", your name and address, and mail to: **In the U.S.:** Silhouette Desire Celebration 1000 Sweepstakes, P.O. Box 9069, Buffalo, N.Y. 14269-9069, or **In Canada:** Silhouette Desire Celebration 1000 Sweepstakes, P.O. Box 637, Fort Erie, Ontario L2A 5X3. Limit one entry per envelope. Entries must be sent via first-class mail and be received no later than 6/30/96. No liability is assumed for lost, late or misdirected mail.

Official Entry Form—Silhouette Desire Celebration 1000 Sweepstakes

Name: _____

Address: _____

City: _____

State/Province: _____

Zip or Postal Code: _____

Favorite Desire Author: _____

Favorite Desire Book: _____

SWEEPS

This July, watch for the delivery of...

An exciting new miniseries that appears in a different Silhouette series each month. It's about love, marriage—and Daddy's unexpected need for a baby carriage!

Daddy Knows Last unites five of your favorite authors as they weave five connected stories about baby fever in New Hope, Texas.

- **THE BABY NOTION** by Dixie Browning
  (SD#1011, 7/96)

- **BABY IN A BASKET** by Helen R. Myers
  (SR#1169, 8/96)

- **MARRIED...WITH TWINS!**
  by Jennifer Mikels
  (SSE#1054, 9/96)

- **HOW TO HOOK A HUSBAND (AND A BABY)**
  by Carolyn Zane
  (YT#29, 10/96)

- **DISCOVERED: DADDY** by Marilyn Pappano
  (IM#746, 11/96)

Daddy Knows Last arrives in July...only from

DKLT

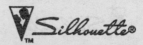